Harmless News in Myrtle Beach

A Journalist Seeks the Truth About UFOs

Larry C. Timbs Jr.

copyright@2022 Larry C. Timbs Jr.
ISBN: 979-8-9860608-4-2

Victoria Fletcher
hootbookspublishing.biz
vfletcher56@gmail.com

Dedication

This book is dedicated to all those hearty souls I served with in air defense in 1968-1969 in the U.S. Air Force in the Philippines.

It was the height of the Vietnam War. And we were responsible—at Clark Air Base and Wallace Air Station—for protecting against any inbound unidentified aircraft.

There were times, ingrained forever in my memory, when the officer in charge of our units, typically a lieutenant or captain, had to make the call on whether to scramble fighter jets. Many times he didn't issue the scramble order although maybe he should have.

Because those inbound blips were potentially deadly—especially the ones coming from Vietnam, China, or south of the Philippines.

My fellow Air Force pals and I were either scope dopes (radar operators), board plotters (think writing backwards and drawing erasable arrows on a big plexiglass grid/map), or we worked in I.D. (where we checked to see if the aircraft had filed a flight plan).

We did what we could, 24/7, to protect freedom and democracy.

More than 50 years later, I still remember those days and nights on the plotting board at the Clark Air Defense Control Center. And how could I ever forget talking to "Musketeer," the call sign for the radar operators at Wallace Air Station at Poro Point?

Fellow former airmen of the Philippines, I hope you will find my novel gives you something to reminisce about.

We are getting gray or bald (those of us still breathing) but we should never forget what we did.

Table of Contents

Chapter 1

Just Another Day At The Paper And Then...

The report was titillating.

It's primary source was Lucille Mulligan—a middle-aged Myrtle Beach woman.

She had sworn to police that she'd been part of something other worldly.

By that, I mean, she and two of her close friends told authorities they had been stopped in their car and abducted—taken up into a hovering disc-shaped glowing craft controlled by creatures that were not human.

"Frightful looking supernatural creatures," they said, that they described in detail to the police.

"They didn't so much as touch us or even say a word to us but it was like they could read our thoughts and knew we were scared to death," were Lucille's words in the police report.

Her two traumatized friends corroborated everything she said. All three of them told of being "beamed up" (their terminology) into the giant, brightly illuminated circular craft that had somehow stopped their car and bathed it in a thick ray of light.

But what to make of this reported strange encounter?

There are no secrets in a moderate-sized South Carolina town. Within two hours of the police report being filed—and before any reporter had a chance to read it—tongues began to wag.

Some locals spoke of the three women being taken aboard a flying saucer by aliens from another galaxy.

Staunch believers of the incredible tale included Lucille and her two companions in the 2002 Toyota Camry that night—Maxine Robinson and Ida Mae James. Several close, longtime acquaintances of the three "abductees" also made it known that these were good, salt-of-the-earth Christian women who had never been known to tell a lie.

Many of the believers attended Sunday School and Bible study classes with Lucille, Maxine, and Ida Mae or worked diligently on church fundraisers with them. Many were also always the first to volunteer to help a distraught congregant in crisis. And to declare that they believed and trusted one another unconditionally was a vast under-statement.

They were threads of the same cloth.

Soulmates bound together by their close friendship and by the rock of their faith—the First Baptist Church Reformed of the Grand Strand.

As I read again the police report of their sworn statements that the three of them separately corroborated under hypnosis two days later by a state appointed medical professional, I also reminded myself of the skeptics.

And there were plenty of those in and around Myrtle Beach.

People who made no secret of announcing that the three so-called abductees had cooked up a wildly fantastic story just to see how many gullible, ignorant people would swallow it.

"I've known Maxine Robinson pert neer all my life, and I ain't afraid to tell ya that she can be a handful," groused 70-year-old Lucius McClain, owner of a hardware store about two miles from the beach.

"Why, did you know she even tried to fire the top doctor in our county? And she didn't just try. She out 'n' out did it—and in front of a bunch of people. The woman downright loves to play to an audience. Has a flair, to say the least, for the dramatic!"

The incident McClain spoke of at the beach community's main medical clinic was well known by many—as the newspaper I reported for had played it up at the time on the front page.

I smiled to myself as I recalled the particulars— which hadn't happened that long ago.

The story appeared under my byline—Lester W. Harmless, general assignment reporter for the Ocean Herald. That title meant I covered just about anything that was newsworthy in our part of coastal South Carolina. The police/crime, city and county government, and medical beats kept me busy most days. And if it were a slow news day—a rarity at our bustling little paper—I busied myself looking through archived local stories from 10, 20, 30 years ago. Because news had a way of repeating itself, and if you knew what happened in the past,

4

you were bound to have a better handle on how to report on the same kind of happening today.

At least that's what my editor-in-chief, Charles W. Wallace, had said to me again and again since I'd been at the paper.

But when the paper got a tip that one Maxine Robinson had flown off into a rage against a respected physician, no one had to ask me twice to pursue it. After all, I thought, *how often is it that a patient overtly challenges the authority, and in front of witnesses no less, of her doctor?*

I soon learned that Maxine had not only erupted in red-hot anger but had done it, in fact, in front of a number of people—in her hospital room at the clinic.

It had been quite the story—with the front-page headline in large type screaming: **LOCAL HEART ATTACK PATIENT FIRES CARDIOLOGIST FROM HER BEDSIDE**

It seemed that the woman, who lived alone, had suffered severe chest pains at about one in the morning at her home. She somehow had managed to drive herself to the ER, where they triaged her and immediately admitted her to the ICU.

The next morning at about 10, her personal physician, Dr. Jacob Forrest, with his stethoscope dangling from his neck and in a starched white jacket, arrived at her bedside. He had arrived at the clinic about two hours earlier and had already seen a dozen patients.

Little did he know what he was walking into when he approached Maxine Robinson's bedside.

He had gotten there not a minute too early, especially if you were to ask his patient, who was livid with anger.

She had reconstructed the entire scene, in detail, for me, and, of course, my ears couldn't get enough of it.

"Why didn't you come see about me last night in the emergency room, when I told 'em to call ya and fetch ya here?!" Maxine, balling her fists and sitting straight up in her bed, had demanded. "I was havin' a heart attack for God's sake!"

Hours later, in her hospital room with her were her long-faced, silver-haired, shell-shocked physician; two registered nurses; a lab technician and her student assistant; an elderly custodian who had just finished mopping the floor and was loading his cart; and a bright-eyed, pony-tailed, high school candy striper.

The angry patient, unabashed, played to the stunned onlookers as a Dr. Forrest bewildered began fiddling with his tie and mumbled something about whether she was absolutely sure she had suffered a heart attack.

"You're damn right I had a heart attack!" she yelled, loud enough that those passing by in the hallway, as well as staff at the nursing station farther away, could hear.

"And you call yourself a doctor! Why, you're nothin' but a fake in a white jacket. Don't even think about touchin' me and get the hell outta my room right now! You're fired!"

As the humiliated M.D. gathered his wits, made a weak attempt at an apology, waved farewell, and shriveled out of the room, those who witnessed the episode said nothing.

Had the aggrieved woman actually refused the care of one of the community's most respected physicians?

And had she, to boot, fired him?

"Can you actually fire your doctor?" one startled nurse at the clinic whispered a few minutes after the incident. "Don't you have to go through some kind of medical board or something?"

"He was gettin' too big for his britches anyways," another nurse offered. "And he was takin' a likin' to those sweet young student nurses. But God Almighty, please don't ever tell him I said that. I have to work here. I need my job."

So most of this—which I had woven into my front-page news story—was in the back of my mind as I began contemplating how I'd pursue the tale of these three women. They'd told the fantastically unbelievable or potentially believable (depending on your mindset) narrative of being stopped and taken aboard a spacecraft commandeered by aliens.

First, however, I'd have to convince my editor that it was actually a legitimate story that deserved our attention.

Which I knew would not be easy.

Chapter 2
Convincing The Gatekeeper

So, copy of the police report in hand, I made my way back to the Ocean Herald newsroom and tapped on my editor's office door.

Behind me in a huge, open-aired space, in a beehive of activity, reporters were busily at work. Some wore headsets or spoke softly in phones. Some paced nervously and wrung their hands, as if trying to summon another ounce of creative juice. Others just sat silent staring at their notes, deciding apparently how they would shape what they were about to write. Running throughout all of it were ringing phones and the steady clickity-clack of fingers on computer keyboards.

"Come on in!" Charles W. Wallace beckoned.

Wallace, a crusty old hard-core editor-in-chief was sipping on a cup of coffee and reviewing a rundown of stories and pictures scheduled for publication the next day. Sweat soaked the armpits of what likely had been a starched, collared shirt earlier that day. A leaking ballpoint pen had stained the top of his left shirt pocket with blue ink. What

9

hours earlier had been a crisply, neatly tied tie had come unraveled.

"What's up, Harmless?" he barked as he sat his coffee cup next to a framed photo of his favorite pet—a 10-year-old Shetland sheep dog named Roadie.

"Make it quick whatever it is, cause I've got a damn staff meeting in 10 minutes. They've gone meeting crazy around this joint."

"Well, sir," I replied, "I've come across something a few hours ago at the police department. It's pretty incredible. I just want to run it by you before I pursue it."

"So what the hell is it?" Wallace snarled. "You got another report of a man gettin' his arm bitten off by an alligator while tryin' to get his golf ball out of a water hazard?

"Or was some son-of-a-bitch wadin' waist high in the surf and a shark took a chunk 'a flesh outta him?

"Or, even better yet, another piece about a guy dropping his credit card at a fast-food drive through and getting crushed when he bent down to pick it up?

"Tell me you gotta genu-INE story, Harmless! That's the lifeblood of this newspaper. A God-forsaken REAL story that makes people gasp or say, "Oh shit!"

"You got an 'Oh Shit' story, young man?"

I swallowed hard, gathered my wits, and gritted my teeth, knowing full well that what I was about to say would be a hard sell.

And then I said it.

"Well, Sir, it seems that we have three women in our community who swear to the police that they've been accosted by aliens in some sort of craft from outer space."

My boss said nothing, but his jaws seemed to tighten and his forehead furrowed.

"And that's not the half of it," I added. "All three of them have told the same story under hypnosis— that they were on their way back from a short road trip out of town a couple of nights ago when their car suddenly lost power and a bright, hovering, circular object…"

"Just end it right there, Harmless!" Wallace interrupted. He was grimacing. "You're trying to make me believe some kind of hogwash about a flying saucer?!

"You want me to be the laughingstock of this town, let alone this newsroom? You think I was born yesterday? Why that's the oldest lie in the books.

"Flying freakin' saucers—really? Aliens? Little green men from another planet?"

"But Sir, please let me finish. This story already has legs. Folks're talkin' about it at the county clerk's office. I was just there this morning, in fact, and what's on file at the police department travels like lightning. You can't keep a lid on something like this. It'll be on the local TV CBS affiliate by tomorrow morning, if not by tonight.

"With all due respect, Sir, this is red hot."

"I don't care if it's a pot boiling over!" Wallace shot back. Straightening his tie and then stroking his mustache, the hard-nosed, beady-eyed editor stared angrily at me. It was an exasperated look that I'd seen before and had vowed that I wouldn't again trigger. An expression that meant I'd best end this conversation right now and exit stage left. "You got anything else, Harmless? Maybe something about a werewolf?"

Wallace took his jacket from off the top of a clothes' rack in one corner of his office and began wriggling into it.

But not before curling his nose up at me and motioning me toward the door.

"Well, Sir, I'll just be on my way, then. I just wanted to let you know the latest. Forgive me if I've wasted your time."

"You know what, Harmless?" said the editor, forcing a slight smile. "For all your minuses, you still have the makings of a good journalist. You know how to write and you have a nose for what people want to know about—most of the time. I'm not giving up on you at all. Just remember what they taught you about that concept called 'news' in journalism school. What we're about at this newspaper is covering and uncovering the truth about what's happening day in and day out.

"Nothing more and nothing less. Just the truth, the whole truth, and nothing but the truth. Same as how they put it in a courtroom. Like they always said it on that Perry Mason TV show. Just try to remember that, will ya?"

"Yes Sir," I replied meekly, although I had no idea of who Perry Mason was. "I'll be on my way now and let you get to your staff meeting. Have a good rest of the day, Sir."

I left the editor's spacious, glassed-in office, with its overstuffed plush swiveling chair, and returned to my workstation—an 80 square foot threadbare cubby hole with a hard-back chair and a simple metal desk littered with a jumble of pocket-sized reporters' note pads, audio recorders, cell phones, and pens piled here and there next to my computer.

I sat down and began planning how I'd write tomorrow's update about incidents reported to the Myrtle Beach Police Department.

There had been a breaking and entering at a beachside residence, along with a woman who'd reported a man tried to assault her while she strolled late one evening on a pier.

Also on the police blotter: a distressed farmer who'd lost 15 of his cows in a thunderstorm when lightning struck them as the frightened animals huddled beneath a live oak tree.

Why that had been reported to police, I wasn't sure, but it was still worth noting when I wrote my daily roundup from the blotter.

And lastly, police had responded to a call that someone had thoughtlessly left a small dog in the back seat of a locked car when coastal temperatures had soared to 95 degrees. Law enforcement had gotten there just in the nick of time to break a window and save the dog which, if paramedics were to be believed, wouldn't have survived another 30 minutes.

And then, of course, there was the police report of the three women's encounter with that strange round object and creatures from God knows where.

That was a report I definitely would NOT pursue or write about for my upcoming police update story.

Not worth getting on the bad side of editor-in-chief Charles W. Wallace, who'd made it crystal clear that nothing pertaining to flying saucers, extraterrestrials, Bigfoot, vampires, or any other seemingly unbelievable activity would see the light of day in his newspaper.

Wallace's stern admonition echoed through my mind as I considered again that strange encounter the three women said they had. And not only strange, but out-of-this-world bizarre and curious.

"Always be a skeptic, Harmless," the editor had preached. "Anybody can say anything or write anything but that doesn't mean it's true. If your mother says she loves you, check it out!"

To my way of thinking, my boss had been too quickly dismissive of a reported happening that even now would be the talk of Myrtle Beach. And I could well imagine how it was bound to play on social media. You couldn't suppress something this sensational.

It didn't have to be real to be news, in my opinion, as long as people talked about it, used it to feed the gossip mill, chatted it up in barber shops or beauty salons, or whispered about it around workplace water coolers.

Still, I reminded myself who I worked for: the esteemed and powerful Mr. Wallace. My fate, and to some degree, my future as a journalist, rested in his hands.

Best, for the time being, to play it safe and stick to writing about what people expected to read—and not give them something that would only shock or maybe even scare them.

Chapter 3
Pursuing The Story

Things changed—and very quickly—that same evening, less than 72 hours after the reported sighting and abduction of Lucille and her two friends.

The first sense I got that we at the newspaper couldn't just dismiss the report as fiction or mindless gossip was a long phone message left on my cell phone's voice mail:

"Hey, Lester, I heard y'all are sittin' on a whale of a big story at the newspaper. Coverin' it up, actually. Who or what are y'all tryin' to protect? What happened ta Lucille and Maxine and Ida Mae oughta get any journalist's blood pumpin'!

"Why, I was at prayer meetin' tonight and ya know what's on everybidy's mind? Well, unfortunately, it ain't Jesus or John the Baptist. Nope, not at all. It's that UFO and them creatures that captured three of our own and, thank God, didn't hurt 'em! Now, that's a damned, rip-roarin' good story, Lester.

18

Don't cha think? Do you remember what news is, my man?

"Can't wait to read about it in the Ocean Herald. Tomorrow, Lester. And if it's not in there, you'll have a ton'a angry readers."

Not leaving his name, the caller then abruptly hung up.

Okay, so a curious or nosy reader heard about the police report. So what? That still doesn't make it bonafide news. Nope. Not at all according to editor-in-chief, Charles W. Wallace.

But turns out that wasn't my only voicemail on the subject. Checking my cell phone more closely, I discovered I had 15 more messages—each of which had essentially the same content and some had the demanding (borderline insulting) tone as the first.

But, then again, I figured a busybody could have orchestrated all those. Maybe a class of students or group or club. I had learned long ago that people're like sheep. Ask them to sign a petition or join a cause and most will, without so much as a moment's hesitation. Maybe that was what was at play here. Maybe some nut had gotten wind of that police report and started a campaign against the newspaper. Still didn't necessarily make for legitimate news. Might be somebody's just trying to embarrass our paper.

Trying to get my mind thinking about other things, I quit listening to the voicemails and turned on my TV to catch the 6 o'clock news on the local CBS affiliate.

I got the customary introductory upbeat music and the video of ocean waves crashing against the shoreline followed by the two anchors giving a brief rundown of what would be aired on the upcoming newscast.

The senior anchor, a distinguished looking middle-aged guy named Bob Gibson, teased: "And tonight, live from Surfside Beach, we have Nicole Kennedy reporting on a strange sighting. Seems a surf fisherman saw something very mysterious in the sky."

"That's right, Bob," the female TV reporter eagerly chimed in from the beach, just a few feet from the waves. And that fisherman wasn't the only person to report seeing something strange. Since I've been down here today, I've spoken to about 20 people who say they witnessed the same thing.

"The same thing in the sky, that is, that surf fisherman, Barry Gray and his wife of 35 years, Becky Gray, told me about. They were standing pretty near where I'm standing right now trying their luck casting out into these very waves that you see behind me, hoping for a bite from maybe a Spanish mackerel or even a flounder.

"Mr. and Mrs. Gray (camera angle moves from the reporter to the couple who'd been fishing), could you tell us what you saw just before you reeled your lines in?"

"Well," an elderly Mr. Gray pauses, wiping the salty sweat from his forehead, "it was something I don't think me and the Mrs. here'll ever forget. We'd been fishin' for goin' on two hours and hadn't had much luck so we'd decided to pack our gear and head home. We began pulling our lines back in."

"And then, Mr. Gray, what exactly did you notice up above?" the TV reporter asked. She had her microphone pressed in the man's face.

"I reckon Becky 'n' me both seen something up in the sky that we'll never forget."

"And what was it that you saw, Mr. Gray?"

21

"They were two flyin' objects—pretty big actually—that were close together, about a thousand feet over the ocean. And they weren't so much as flyin' as they was just hangin' real still, like in one place.

"Big, round, 'flamin' orange balls is how I'd describe 'em. Just hangin' there right still like in the sky, and then lickity split they was gone.

"Never seen the like of it in my life.

"And guess what? Five minutes or so later they appeared again—in the same area, but closer to the surface of the ocean. They didn't stay long this time."

Becky Gray said, "I tried to get a picture of 'em but they were too fast."

"Faster'n a bolt of lightnin'," her husband added. "They were there over the water and then they took off and we ain't seen hide ner hair of 'em since."

Her interest building, the reporter asked the couple to estimate the size of the orange balls.

"About as big as a jumbo jet, only round. I mean, my gosh, they was quite a sight!"

"I just wish I'd gotten a picture cause I know it's hard to believe," his wife, her eyes widening, added. "I was sa nervous I couldn't find my cell phone."

The attractive young TV reporter thanked the couple and began her sign-off.

"And that's tonight's lead story, Bob and Lisa, from Surfside Beach. What exactly was it in the sky that Mr. and Mrs. Gray saw? We'll be following this story closely and reaching out to the folks in the air traffic control tower at the airport for a comment. More about the strange sighting tonight at 11 on, as we always say, News That Matters. This is Nicole Kennedy reporting for WJHZ TV channel 23."

When my cell phone buzzed, I muted the newscast.

It was Rose Jansen, clerk for our newsroom.

Rose, in her mid-60s and at the paper for the last three decades, kept regular tabs on the breaking news of the day or night and routed phone calls to reporters, photographers, and editors. She was the general go-to person at the paper when it came to supplying background or historical context to anything newsworthy.

In other words, as some of the veteran journalists at the Ocean Herald put it, she knew where the bodies were buried.

Whereas some in the newsroom were bothered that "Nosey Rosey" (as they called her) always seemed to be looking over their shoulder, they were in the minority.

As for me and many other journalists at the paper, Rose had more than once been a lifesaver. If she sensed that a reporter was pursuing a wild goose chase, she'd advise him or her to spend their time on something more productive. Likewise, if one of us tasked with covering the daily news overlooked a source or news angle that Rose valued highly, she had a way of steering the affected journalist in the right direction. And she could spot a hole in a news story a mile away and wasn't shy about telling a reporter or editor that it needed to be filled.

She came to be lovingly known by her admirers as the paper's "institutional suppository" inasmuch as she'd saved many a journalist's ass from troubled waters.

"Lester, did you happen to hear about the reported sighting of UFOs at Surfside Beach?

"This is Rose, by the way, and I'm sorry to bother you at home, but did you catch the local news this evening? And if you didn't watch the news, have you checked your Facebook page or Instagram within the last few hours?"

Rose doesn't miss a beat, I thought. *She hears and see all.*

"If you're referring to the eyewitnesses' reports of strange objects seen hovering over the ocean just off Surfside Beach, yep, I'm in the loop about that, Rose. But I brought that sighting up earlier today with the boss and he waved me off the story."

"Does he have any earthly idea how friggin' BIG a story this already is?" Rose growled. "Would Charles W. Wallace know a story if one bit him in his big fat butt? Does the man have an ounce of a brain in his head?"

Not knowing exactly how to respond, I said as little as possible—something to the effect that I was low on the totem pole in the newsroom and just wanted to stay out of trouble.

I thanked Rose for calling me and promised her I'd revisit the idea of a story about the mysterious sighting as soon as possible.

Meaning I didn't intend to bring it up again unless the boss changed his mind and couldn't stand being scooped by TV news, social media addicts, bloggers, or anyone else with a keyboard in cyberspace.

That evening, I tuned to the late-night TV newscast, which rehashed what had been broadcast earlier about the UFOs. I also spent time on the Internet, researching reports of what were being called "unidentified aerial phenomena."

I gathered that was currently the preferred term— our government's lingo—instead of "UFO" for unknown objects in the sky that people had sworn they'd seen.

And there apparently had been hundreds of such sightings—from credible witnesses throughout the world.

What they reported hovering just above trees or streaking across the sky ran the gamut from being shaped like discs, triangles, cigars, and more recently tic tacs (like the breath mints you buy at the store).

Some, like a well-known 2004 sighting by two U.S. Navy fighter pilots flying off the coast of San Diego, had been captured on radar.

That particular encounter, not publicly disclosed till 2020, had the objects flying at speeds of up to 24,000 miles per hour.

And not only did the unidentified tic tac shaped aerial objects manifest such hypersonic speed, they did it without leaving a contrail or any other evidence of propulsion.

Such reports had captured the imagination of millions of Americans—so much so that the U.S. federal government had been pressured into taking action.

No longer, within the last couple of years, did the Pentagon and U.S. intelligence community dismiss UFO sightings as absurd. Rather, there was movement toward taking the entire subject more seriously.

Respected senators like Marco Rubio of Florida and the late John McCain of Arizona had said that unidentified aircraft in American airspace represented a potential threat to national security. Even a former U.S. president—Barack Obama— had said in a widely published interview that the astounding movement and trajectory of unidentified aerial phenomena could not be explained. Furthermore, he fully supported the idea of our government investigating and getting to the bottom of what had intrigued so many Americans.

I kept reading and looking at the videos on YouTube and the more I delved into the topic, the more curious I became.

Of course, the million-dollar question always boiled down to this: Are UFO's evidence of alien life?

And closely related to that: Are we earthlings alone in this vast universe? Is there someone or something else out there that keeps visiting us?

Chapter 4
The Story Begins To Get Legs

I read about UFOs until I was blurry eyed, then drifted off to slumberland.

I got awakened early the next morning by the chirpy, upbeat sound of the lead-in to the 7 o'clock local TV news broadcast. I had set an electronic timer on my TV for the morning newscast to wake me up.

"Good morning, everyone. Lisa, I understand that we have a live follow-up report from our very own Nicole Kennedy about that reported UFO sighting at Surfside Beach yesterday," the senior news anchor teased.

"That's correct, Bob. Nicole reached out to the director of the air traffic control tower at the international airport. She got his take on what that couple and many others at the beach said they saw. Here she is with her latest report."

"Thank you, Bob and Lisa. If you saw my earlier interview with Mr. Barry Gray and his wife Becky Gray, you'll recall that they'd been fishing at

Surfside Beach. Well, they didn't catch anything out of the ocean but they sure said they saw something mysterious above the ocean.

"The Grays said they saw two big ball-shaped flying orange objects. Furthermore the man and his wife said the objects hovered in the sky for a short time, before zipping away faster than you can imagine over the horizon. Then, minutes later, the objects zipped right back to where they'd been before and stayed there, just above the ocean, ever so briefly before leaving again.

"And the Grays weren't alone in vowing they'd witnessed something mysterious in the sky. While I was interviewing them, many others at the beach vouched for them.

"We're absolutely certain that we saw a UFO," one man told me as I began walking back to our news van. He had been scouring the beach with a metal detector.

"Which brings me to my interview with Ted Staley, director of the air traffic control tower at Myrtle Beach International Airport.

"Mr. Staley, preferring not to appear on camera, would not confirm or deny that there had been unidentified flying objects in the sky near the beach earlier today.

"But he did tell me that the radar in the airport's air traffic control tower had, in fact, detected aerial phenomena for which they couldn't account. It hadn't interfered with any incoming or outgoing flights at the airport, so he'd seen no need to ask the Air Force to scramble jets.

"But now, with reports of the Surfside Beach unknown phenomena or UFOs or whatever you want to call them mushrooming on social media, Mr. Staley said he's having second thoughts.

"He's forwarding an electronic record of that airport's tower radar detection to the commander of the 118th fighter squadron at Charleston Air Force Base. We'll stay on this story, Bob and Lisa, and let you know when the Air Force responds.

"Meanwhile, this is Nicole Kennedy, reporting live for News That Matters, WJHZ TV channel 23."

Back to news anchor Bob Gibson: "This is a story that has generated a lot of public interest and we here at the station will stay on top of. We will keep reaching out for comment from the Air Force, the local police, and from others as the situation warrants. Stay tuned to this station, WJHZ TV channel 23, for more details as they become available."

And with that promise of more to come on a story that was bound to have captivated thousands living on the Grand Strand of South Carolina, the news station shifted to what it always seemed to cover nightly and daily: saltwater fishing reports, tourism tendencies, economic development, beach and tidal notes, the latest surge of the coronavirus, political squabbling over a proposed new interstate highway, crime, and court trials.

The TV station also spotlighted the ongoing tremendous growth of housing and businesses on and near the Grand Strand. For what had one time been a sleepy little coastal county of about 75,000 people in 1985 had mushroomed to a population of 345,000 in 2021.

"They won't be satisfied till they cut every tree down in Horry County," one old-timer groused. "They're making way for all these people from the Northeast who're taking over what used to be the best part of our state."

I smiled to myself each time I thought about that. No way, I figured, would our beach community ever stop growing. In fact, it was just the opposite. People were moving in here by the droves, many of them from places like New York, New Jersey, Connecticut, Pennsylvania, and Maryland.

And they all seemed to want the same thing: a warm climate, which we offered for about 10 months out of the year, golf courses (we had about 90 of those), low taxes, and affordable housing.

For sure, our taxes and home prices were low compared to what folks confronted in places like New York and New Jersey.

Because I had heard from more than one New York transplant brag that for the same money he could buy twice or three times the house here that he had in New York.

And the property taxes here? They were downright miniscule compared to what you paid in New England—often less than one-fourth of what you paid up north.

And then, last but not least, we had 60 miles of beautiful beaches—the main reason, in my opinion, that people relocated here.

Why go all the way to Florida when you could find a little corner of beach paradise in Myrtle Beach, South Carolina? So we had it all: the magnificent Atlantic Ocean with all its mighty waves, the sand and invigorating salt air, temperate climate, entertainment and dining options galore, abundant wildlife including some of the best fishing on the East Coast, a quality affordable lifestyle, and things to do and see and enjoy aplenty.

Little wonder, I thought, that we were one of the fastest growing counties in America. I had even recently heard that we were the fastest growing county east of the Mississippi River. The news was out. We had lots to offer and the inflow of folks from the North, some of whom complained that the locals were backward, ignorant, provincial, and unfriendly, wasn't likely to stop anytime soon, if ever. In fact, in some ways, our part of the state wasn't like any other part of South Carolina. It wasn't really South Carolina; I had reminded myself many times. Actually more like little New York or little New Jersey with so many of the transplants from those states.

Not that Myrtle Beach, the town with hundreds of pancake houses, was without its challenges. The entire area, which some critics said was nothing but a big swamp, suffered from drainage problems, too many people living in too small an area, encroachment of wildlife stemming from overdevelopment, so much clearcutting of forests that at least one northern transplanted resident said it rivaled Sherman's scorched earth policy, a severe labor shortage—causing many restaurants and motels to close early or offer reduced services—and aging roads, bridges, and other forms of infrastructure that were fast becoming inadequate.

Even rentals were beginning to become out of reach. Beach houses were going for $500 to $600 a night in the peak summer months. And if you wanted a decent permanent rental anywhere near the beach, a tiny 900 square foot apartment with one bathroom went for at least $1,500 a month. Expensive and cramped, especially if you had a family.

On that note, my mind drifted again to the idea that strange creatures from afar somewhere out there in the depths of the universe had also found our community.

If this were actually the case, who were they exactly and what did they want, if anything?

And what journalist would be the first in history to make contact with them?

I turned the TV off, got caught up on all my unread text messages and e-mails, and turned my attention to more mundane terrestrial tasks—like writing an update of the local court docket and the latest health department inspection scores of restaurants.

It wasn't glamorous journalism but someone still had to do it. And along with the other routine reporting I had to do, it made for a long, trying day. I was too bushed to even watch the local TV news that night, so I hit the hay early.

Chapter 5

Someone Smart About Things In The Sky

Out of bed at 6:30 the next morning and in and out of the shower within three minutes, I dressed, brewed myself a cup of strong coffee, and ate a toasted cinnamon raisin bagel with cream cheese.

It promised to be a busy day as I had notes on a number of pieces I needed to review and turn into publishable articles—or at least material ready for editing and revision.

While I thought about that, I also wondered about the newscast two nights previously—with the TV news reporter promising to stay on the story about the huge glowing objects. Dozens of people had now come forward pledging that they'd seen something they'd never forget in the sky. And I was sure that social media chatter on the strange aerial craft—or whatever they were—was by now off the charts.

Still, even the testimony of numerous reliable eyewitnesses wouldn't change the hardened mind of my doubting editor. It'd take something really dramatic, some sort of tangible evidence, if there could be such a thing, in this situation, for him to come around.

Meanwhile, I got a tone on my iPhone. It was a text message from Rose, the news clerk, instructing me to call my editor ASAP.

Well, maybe the old war horse has seen the light at last, I thought.

But alas, I'd been too quick to give him the benefit of the doubt.

Instead, my assignment this morning was to drive out to the residence of Dr. and Mrs. Henry Evans, who lived a few miles from the beach in a community called Socastee. I recognized the names from a piece the paper had done six months ago on their son, young Justin Evans, at the time about 9 years old, if memory served me correct.

I pulled up the article on my phone to refresh my memory. Dr. Evans was a tenured professor in the Department of Astronomy at nearby Coastal Carolina University. His wife Nora worked as a registered nurse at the well-respected Grand Strand Medical Center, the main acute health care facility at the beach.

So, a nice upper-middle class Grand Strand family. Justin, their son, had been severely injured when his dad, with his only son sitting gleefully behind him, had lost control of the family's riding lawnmower.

The mower flipped over, with dad jumping off just in the nick of time and escaping injury.

However, Justin, covered in blood and screaming, had almost died. He'd landed squarely under the cutting blades of the powerful mower, and the sharpened steel had done a number, and then some, on his face and head.

But thanks to quick response from paramedics and an air evacuation flight to Duke University Pediatric Center, a team of medical professionals had saved his life.

According to a follow-up story a few weeks later, he was beginning to talk again, drink and eat soft food, but barely because of the severe injuries to his mouth, lips, nose, jawbone, and teeth.

Pediatric neurosurgeons at Duke had worked on him for 17 hours in the OR, doing their best to reconstruct the child's damaged facial bones and fractured skull.

They had worked a miracle, apparently.

400 stitches and weeks of rehab later and with lots of well wishes and prayers from a supportive close-knit beach community, Dr. and Mrs. Evans brought their only child back home.

And so now, my task was to visit the Evans family, find out how they were doing and do a quick interview with Justin, if he felt up to it.

Hopefully, my efforts would culminate in one of those feel-good, uplifting, human interest feature stories that most readers said they loved to read.

Accompanying me to the Evans home was one of our newsroom's photographers, the grizzled, obese but thoroughly competent Robert Carter.

A Carolinas Panthers cap on his head and wearing a beach t-shirt, faded jeans, and snakeskin boots, Carter had won hundreds of awards for his work. Maybe the most awards of any news photographer in South Carolina. And he'd recently been nominated for a Pulitzer Prize for his series of photos of an ex-con tobacco farmer and his family in a nearby county.

You hardly ever saw him without his grab bag of cameras, telephoto and wide-angle lenses, and tripod. Today was no exception as the always-prepared photojournalist had the tools of his trade.

We pulled into the driveway of the Evans two-story brick residence and I made a quick note of their property. It was easily a million-dollar home, with a well-manicured luscious sloping lawn framed by azaleas, camelias, Indian Hawthorns, butterfly bushes, and crepe myrtles. Two 25-foot-high palm trees were on each side of the entrance to the main driveway. And to one side of the beautiful house stood a giant live oak tree, Spanish moss hanging from its gnarled limbs. The magnificent tree, with a diameter of about four feet, had obviously withstood many a hurricane.

Parked in front of the double garage were a late-model BMW convertible and a Mercedes Benz. The Mercedes looked like it came right out of the showroom.

The Evans couple did pretty well for themselves, I decided. I suspected that once I was inside their home, I'd see they had finely appointed name-brand furniture, new appliances, either shiny hardwood floors or expensive Persian carpets, and granite kitchen counters.

And I was right on the money. They had all that and more, including brightly colored curtains accentuating every window, what appeared to be a fully stocked bar, and one of the biggest flat screen TVs I'd ever seen mounted on their living room wall.

Dr. Evans, shaking my hand and also making my photographer feel welcome, said, "Come on into our cozy abode."

If you didn't know him, you might guess he was a college professor. He was broad shouldered and balding, had piercing darkish brown eyes, and a neatly trimmed beard. He appeared to be a tad over 6 feet tall and I figured he'd been a star athlete back in the day.

But for now, he definitely had that genteel, professorial look, complete even with the patches on the elbows of his corduroy sports jacket.

He said, "My wife is upstairs for a few minutes with our son, Justin, but she'll join us soon. Meanwhile, would either one of you like some kind of refreshment? We have ice cold Coca-Cola, root beer, lemonade, iced tea, and the list goes on. Let me know your pleasure."

We thanked him for the offer but said we were a bit pushed for time (which we were) and asked if we could ask a few questions—on the record—for a story the newspaper wished to publish on their son's recovery.

He said of course we could and invited us to ask he and his wife and son anything.

"But first, if I may, I'd like to tell both of you a few things—a sort of gentle request to how my wife and I'd like you to proceed today. Is that ok?"

We nodded that it was. We were in his home, after all, and only there at his family's pleasure.

He responded: "Well, please take a seat over there, then, and we'll get started."

He directed us to a sectional sofa about 35 feet long and 4 feet wide that had plush, luxurious pillows scattered throughout its sitting and back rest areas. Behind the sofa was a huge saltwater aquarium ablaze with colorful creatures from the sea including gobies, damselfish, lionfish, queen angels, and coral beauties.

As I sank into the sofa and stole one last glance at the fish, they seemed to sense my presence, stirred about (as if showing off), and swam to the top of the surface.

"Quite a collection of fish you have there, Sir," photojournalist Carter said. "They're spectacular."

Dr. Evans grinned and said the fish were his son's favorite pets, especially since the accident, and that he, his wife, and the boy often found peace and happiness in communing with them.

"And how, exactly, does one commune with a fish, Dr. Evans, if I may ask?" I said.

"By doing precisely nothing at all and by just staring at them and letting them know that you are amazed at their beauty and playful spirit," the professor responded. "I have to say, they have been extremely therapeutic for all of us, throughout all this, and we are definitely better off for being near them."

The photographer and I nodded that we understood (although I don't think we really did) and changed the subject to a majestic seascape painting that hung on the wall facing us.

"That has to be the beach at Myrtle Beach State Park, one of my favorite places around here," I said. "I go there often to gaze at the ocean and wildlife."

"Indeed. It's one of our favorites, too," Dr. Evans said. "Did you know the park was built in 1936 by the CCC under the auspices of then-President Franklin Roosevelt? And Roosevelt himself was here to dedicate the park. It's one of his least known legacies in our little coastal community.

"But what I wanted to chat to both of you about has to do with the reason you're here today—to do a follow-up article about my son and his recovery, which I'm glad you're doing because my wife Nora and I have gotten a lot of questions of late about Justin."

Other than encouraging the professor to continue, we said nothing.

And then Nora, her upstairs business with her son apparently completed, joined us.

She was an attractive woman, perhaps in her early 50s, with slightly graying shoulder-length brown hair, perfect teeth, and light blue eyes. She had obviously taken care of herself physically—likely, I supposed, a member of a fitness center—because

45

she had not one ounce of fat, nothing even approaching a sagging belly, and her arms and legs were muscular without seeming overly so. She had a shapely figure and was dressed in a short white skirt and halter, as if she'd just returned from playing tennis.

In short, Nora Evans, R.N., was quite a dish, making Dr. Henry Evans a very lucky man.

"Henry, I trust you've made our guests feel welcome," she began, after introducing herself.

Her blue eyes locked on ours and she continued, "We are honored that you are taking the time and energy to help tell our family's complete story—or at least the part that no one's told up to this point."

I smiled and said: "Well, we are just happy that you thought of our newspaper first, apparently, when you decided you wanted to go public with what has happened since the accident."

"And that brings me to why you are here today," the professor's wife said, eyeballing me and then glancing at the photographer.

"You see, gentlemen, we have this situation with our son, which I'm sure you can appreciate. We've all been through quite a lot, especially Justin."

I nodded my understanding.

"And Justin, whom you'll meet in a few minutes, has made tremendous progress—medically, physically, and emotionally."

Professor Evans put his arm around his wife and hugged her slightly.

Then, lowering his voice, he spoke.

"What Nora's saying is that while Justin has been very brave and made huge strides in his rehab, he's still, yet today, got a ways to go."

The man paused before continuing.

"By that, my wife and I mean that we've had to take some exceptional steps to protect him—to make sure he doesn't regress, as it were."

I nodded sympathetically, then asked him to continue.

"Well, for example, we've removed the mirror in Justin's bedroom and have taken down all the mirrors in the house.

"Our son doesn't need to dwell on his face, although I will note that his surgeons did an amazing job saving his life and reconstructing the bones and tissue in his jaw, nose, cheeks, and lips.

"The mower also did a number on his upper neck and chin, and the doctors at Duke Hospital didn't just stitch him up. As one of them put it, they worked their tails off in that OR putting Humpty Dumpty back together again. I think they're the best plastic surgeons on the planet."

His wife intervened: "But it's going to take a long time for Justin's scars and wounds to fully heal. He may be looking at more surgery. We don't know at this point. Meanwhile, we're doing everything we can to keep him positive.

"Our son is being home schooled but lately he's been asking about when he can return to his normal school. So we've got that, along with other things to deal with, to help make sure he stays on the road to recovery."

"Not an easy task, I'm sure," I allowed.

"So, all that said," Professor Evans noted, "you and your photographer are free to have at it with Justin, or with us, or with anything on this property. Go where your news nose takes you but please be mindful to be discreet, especially with regard to photographing our son."

"Perhaps you could just retouch whatever image you take of him," Nora Evans said, a kind of pleading tone in her voice. "A silhouette, maybe, or a profile shot of Justin from a respectful distance?"

"Justin!" The professor yelled toward the upstairs. "You can come down now. The journalists are here to speak with you."

And with that, the 9-year-old boy bounded down the stairs.

He seemed quite normal in every respect—he had thick, uncombed, beautiful blond hair, a scruffy pair of bony knees that looked like he'd been playing in the dirt, and eyes the same shape and color as those of his dad. He wore a t-shirt emblazoned with "Ninja Warrior," baggy shorts, and sneakers without socks.

Justin flashed us a big smile as he extended his hand for a fist pump.

49

And that's when it really hit me how much he must have suffered from the accident.

All his front teeth were missing, and his bottom lip didn't quite match his top one. I wouldn't quite say that lip was deformed or ruined beyond repair but it struck me as something the doctors had somehow patched together with spare tissue.

He had a nose but just barely. Instead of the nostrils being at the bottom of the nose, they were somehow pointed outward about midway up what must have been at one time, pre-accident, a normal nose.

Scars ran from his lower chin to just below his eyes and then resumed up to his forehead. The scars and gashes were fading, yes, but still readily discernible.

I wondered when, if ever, the boy's face would ever look quasi normal.

What more could any plastic surgeon do to make sure no one stared at him?

"Y'all want to see my room?" Justin asked bubbily. The rest of our visit at the Evans home consisted of Justin talking to us about himself and his family and giving us a tour of the entire house including his backyard where he had a basketball goal, an in-ground pool and a huge cascading fountain surrounded by statues of sharks, whales, and dolphins.

When it came to harkening back to what he remembered about the lawnmower accident, he told us where exactly he was sitting on the mower, how it happened, and what he remembered about being flown to Duke in the helicopter.

And he seemed to have a good grasp of how hard his doctors had worked to save him.

Not once did he refer to wanting to look like everyone else.

Which struck me as kind of odd since wouldn't anyone, under the same circumstances, wish to have a normal looking face?

But I didn't push it, instead asking him at length about his everyday routine and his plans and dreams for the future. Photographer Carter snapped hundreds of pictures, which, I had learned long ago, is what photojournalists do. It struck me that they're like blind men with machine guns, shooting here, there and everywhere and hoping for a handful of useable good pictures.

But, honoring his parents' request, he didn't take a single picture of their son.

Which Justin noticed as Carter packed up his gear and he and I bid farewell to his parents and began to leave.

"Take a picture of me!" he boldly declared. "You didn't get a single one of me. I want my picture made."

The professor and his wife just stared at their son. Then they turned to us.

No one said a word.

"Take a picture of Justin," I commanded the photographer.

When he hesitated, I took a camera out of his bag, focused on the boy, and pressed the shutter release—not once but at least six times.

Until Justin smiled at me and gave me a parting fist pump.

Then, while the boy scampered outside, I lowered my voice and told his parents it would all be okay. I would personally handle the picture of Justin and see to it that it was handled discreetly and professionally—consistent with their fervent request.

At that, Professor Evans—he being a key player in his university's department of astronomy—encouraged me to call him soon.

"Because I've heard about all this hullabaloo of what some are calling a spaceship at the beach," he said.

"And I think there might be more to it than meets the eye. So call me and I'll explain."

"I will certainly do that, Sir. You can count on it."

And I thanked he and his wife again for their time.

Chapter 6
Sighting Suddenly Becomes News

The next morning, I had a message soon as I got to my workstation to report to the editor's office.

Which I did, wondering what the heck had I done or not done to get on the bad side of my boss, Charles W. Wallace.

But when I entered his office, I found to my surprise that Wallace was not alone. With him was none other than the esteemed long-time publisher and owner of the Ocean Herald, the honorable Mrs. Barbara Huntington, executive editor Marshal Preminger (who happened to be the publisher's son), and the paper's science editor, Samuel Kent.

Extra chairs had been brought into Wallace's office so that we all had a place to sit.

When I looked sort of askance at why I had been summoned to what was now appearing, by the second, to be some sort of high-level editorial board meeting, Wallace motioned for me to have a seat.

This time Wallace looked fresher, less sweaty, and more together in his appearance. For example, his tie was tied perfectly, his shirt hadn't yet lost its starch, the few strands of hair on his head seemed to have been combed, and even his shoes were shining.

I thought to myself that Wallace had been given notice of this little gathering perhaps late yesterday or early this morning. So he had come prepared and looking his best.

"Well, I guess we're all here now, and we all know one another, so let's get started," Wallace announced, trying his best not to sound overly officious.

Mrs. Huntington, whom I'd met only once before, briefly at an annual Christmas party, nodded toward us and motioned her readiness to begin. If there were such a thing as a publisher's attire, she had it on: a dark blue pin-striped skirt and matching jacket, light red blouse with shiny matching heels, a plain gold necklace, cufflinks in her blouse sleeves, a dazzlingly huge diamond on her ring finger, and white gold earrings completed her ensemble.

No one at the newspaper knew quite what her son's job or responsibility was. We only knew that his massive office, adjoining his mother's, featured an indoor putting green and a large mahogany conference table that never had anything on it. He frequently accompanied his well-known mother to community fundraisers, civic club meetings, and new business ground breakings. Also known was that he was a stickler for dressing professionally (but again, exactly what his profession was no one could say). Today he appeared to be decked out in a brand-new suit that could have come straight from the finest tailor in Italy.

I thought quickly that I probably appeared underdressed. For some reason, I'd picked an old pair of slacks and a shirt just barely a notch above a beach t-shirt as my outfit that morning. My footwear consisted of white New Balance athletic shoes. But at least I was clean and so were my clothes. I had showered that morning, had shaved, and done my best to control my always unkempt hair.

When I entered my boss' office, I had quickly removed my ball cap.

Which had elicited a hint of a smile from the publisher.

Surely she knew that us working stiffs couldn't look like we had just walked out of a high-end men's clothing shop.

Science editor Kent, on the other hand, just looked like he always did. A sort of bland, thin, greying guy with a goatee, he was in an unremarkable plain cotton brown shirt with bow tie and Chino pants.

"We'll try to keep this short and sweet because I know we're all very busy people," editor Wallace began. "But we're here today to discuss and take action editorially, if need be, on a report of what has become the talk of the beach.

"And I'm not talking about Jaws," he continued, cracking a hint of a smile. "I'm rather referring to the report of a mysterious sighting a few days ago in the sky just off the coast of Surfside Beach.

"Are we all on the same page thus far?" he asked.

When we all nodded that we were, the editor continued, but not without first qualifying what was to come next.

"Now, if any of you know me very well, you know that I might be the biggest skeptic in Myrtle Beach, if not in the state of South Carolina. Just because somebody says they've done something or seen something, doesn't make it a fact. I'm not one for spreading lies or false information or rumors, regardless of how sensational they might be.

"In this particular case, we presumably have eyewitnesses who believe—and let me emphasize that word BELIEVE—that they saw something quite amazing. And now, where does that leave this newspaper exactly?"

"With being engaged in a coverup if we don't start reporting this story," science editor Kent immediately opined. "What the hell are we waiting for? This thing has been all over the local TV news, and their viewership ratings, I'm told, are going through the roof!"

Wallace, who had been cool, calm, and collected up to this point in the meeting, suddenly erupted with anger.

Looking straight into Kent's eyes, he said: "It's exactly that sort of sarcastic, devil may care, know-it-all-attitude that can put our newspaper in danger of losing all credibility!

"I might remind you that we are not Facebook and we are not bloggers and we are not Twitter. We stand for the truth. Truth is the holy grail of journalism. I will not stand by and let you or anyone else cavalierly take the Ocean Herald down a path of ruin. And one more thing:"

Wallace paused for maximum effect.

"FLYING SAUCERS MY ASS!" he barked.

Which was an outburst that finally got publisher Barbara Huntington to speak her piece.

"Gentlemen," she said. "Let us respect one another and listen and then come to an informed consensus of what course the Ocean Herald should pursue. This sighting or revelation or whatever you want to call it has become a matter of great concern. It's front and center on people's minds. The question is: How shall our newspaper handle it?"

The science editor said, "I don't see as to how we have a choice, Ma'am. Because if we don't cover what our readers are talking about, in this case becoming consumed about, we'll soon be out of business. I'm not at all saying that we're being taken over by aliens. I'm saying I don't know, and neither does anyone else. So we have to report the story and try to separate truth from fiction. That's why we're here, at least that's why I thought we were here."

Executive editor Preminger glanced at his mother, as if asking for a cue, and when he got nothing, he sighed, dusted off his lapels, removed his spectacles, and began cleaning them with a fine silk handkerchief. His lips didn't move.

Eyes turned back to editor Wallace.

"I've already said my piece," he said, wiping the perspiration from his forehead. "This could very well turn out to be the greatest hoax in the history of humankind, and I want no part of it. Nor do I want this newspaper to get sucked into it."

And then they looked at me.

"Your thoughts, young man?" publisher Huntington asked. "You haven't said anything up to this point."

That's because no one asked me to speak, I thought.

Wallace, who had by now regained his composure, looked at me and his expression said it was all right for me to speak my piece.

"Well, all I know is it's everywhere on social media, and it's leading the news on the local CBS TV affiliate. And I'm getting insulting calls at my home asking why are we sitting on this story.

"So if you're asking me if I think we should pursue it, I'm like Kent. Seems to me we don't have much of a choice in the matter. Especially if we want folks to keep reading our newspaper."

"Thank you, Mr. Harmless," the publisher said, smoothing her skirt and standing up. "I suppose we all know where we stand now, correct? Let's move this story to the front page or at least to a place in the paper where it will get prominent attention, and if it turns out to be false, we'll report it as such. But if it's true, and extraterrestrials have, for whatever reason, seen fit to visit our community, we'll report that, too. Are we all clear about that?"

When no one responded, but at least two heads nodded in agreement, she seemed satisfied and said the meeting was over and that we should all get back to work.

And from that moment on, the Ocean Herald never again totally discounted the possibility that other worldly aliens had made contact with us.

Chapter 7
Dealing With The Pushback

Of the three women who said their car had been rendered powerless that fateful evening by the circular spacecraft in the sky, one of them was now saying nothing.

She was Lucille Mulligan, who, on behalf of her two close friends—Maxine Robinson and Ida Mae James—had gone to the Myrtle Beach Police Department and filed an incident report.

She wished now that she had kept silent.

Because from almost the instant the police report became public knowledge, it had dominated social media.

Lucille, Maxine, and Ida Mae had become bombarded with prying phone calls, emails and snail mail and even approached by insistent strangers who knocked on their doors. Motorists slowing down in front of their homes, and some even pulling into their driveways, honking their horns, and pleading with them to come out and talk.

63

Everyone wanted to know more about exactly what had happened to them.

When they were beamed up into the spacecraft, what was it like?

Had they been stripped and placed on some sort of examining table?

What exactly had the creatures who had captured them done to them? Had they crossed the boundaries of decency?

And what had the creatures looked like? Their color and size? Two arms and two legs? Humanlike or something else entirely different? Extremely large heads with ghostly eyes and thin, spindly bodies— like folks were used to seeing in sci-fi movies?

The questions went on and on, to the point that Lucille decided that enough was enough. She quickly grew tired of the insatiable public curiosity

It became a kind of pressure, an obsessive public fascination if you will, that threatened to overtake forever her, for-the-most-part, mundane life.

Life for her mostly consisted of getting up early each morning, watching the sun rise, rousing her husband out of bed, laying out his clothes, and taking care of her best friend, her loyal dog Sandy, a 13-year-old Collie.

Then she'd put Sandy on his leash and take him for his morning jaunt through the neighborhood: a scattering of run-down trailers with palm trees and golf carts in their front yards. Soon as dog and woman made the loop through the neighborhood, it was back home where she topped off her bird feeders, cleaned up the dog poop from her small backyard (because, no, you couldn't have folks stepping in you know what!), and watered her plants.

After that, she'd brew herself a cup of coffee and catch up on the news on her iPhone. Later in the day, she'd busy herself with light housework, cooking (not a lot because it was just her, her husband, and her dog), and maybe make a trip to the grocery store or post office.

Then, after nap time, she'd get ready for church, if it happened to be on a day when her Bible study class met, and off she'd go in her aging, dented-here-and-there, Toyota Prius.

After class, and before it got dark, she'd be on her way home to catch the 6 o'clock local news on TV.

After a bite to eat with her husband, she'd take Sandy outside one last time to do his business, feed him, and then retire for the evening— a good book on her nightstand and Sandy within a few feet of her lying in his dog bed.

And that, in a nutshell was Lucille's routine.

Not exciting or the least bit adventurous, although she did, from time to time, take Sandy on his leash down to the beach to take in the waves and wind (which always seemed to be refreshing down there).

Now, her peaceful "leave-me-be" predictable existence seemed threatened.

Whereas, she had never much gravitated toward people—and in fact, liked animals and nature better—now people seemed to be almost moving in on her.

And not only that—they were the worst kind of people. The kind that would keep pounding on your door and calling you and bothering you wherever you went because you, presumably, had been at the center of a once-in-a-lifetime out of this world event.

**

But whereas Lucille quickly sensed which way the wind was blowing and decided suddenly to speak no more of the "incident," Maxine and Ida Mae continued to talk.

It was as if their newly found notoriety had given meaning to their heretofore boring lives, and they vowed to make the most of it.

And why not? they reasoned.

After all, the way they saw it, they'd had no choice in the matter.

To their way of thinking, something extraordinary—no, not just extraordinary but AMAZINGLY AND MIRACULOUSLY RARE AND EXCITING—had happened to them.

And now, understandably, the world wanted to hear all about it—or so they thought.

Because what red blooded human being wouldn't want to know the nitty gritty of all that happened that night?

Lucille, however, continued to stand her ground. She'd had quite enough of the endless questions and public appetite for what was being widely touted in social media as "an alien abduction."

And when one day, out of the blue, someone left a voicemail calling her an out and out liar, that was the proverbial straw that broke the camel's back.

"I knew your daddy and your daddy's daddy, and they were nothing but bald-faced liars. And you're just nothing but a chip off the old block," was the message, left by an elderly male.

So Lucille had had enough. No more trying to respond to every Tom, Dick, and Harry with their endless questions and, increasingly, of late, insinuations that the three women had imagined the entire alien encounter—for the sake of public attention and fascination.

If I knew then what I know now, I'd a never had the police file that incident report, Lucille thought, peeking through a window as three cars, necks craning out of their side windows, lined up in front of her residence.

"Come on out! We know you're in there!" a man with tattoos all over his forearms yelled. "I brung my kids down here all the way from Florence. They want ta hear your whole story about them space aliens."

Lucille drew here drapes closer together and made sure all her windows and doors were locked.

Because you never knew, she thought, *just how far some people would go to get what they wanted.*

Maxine and Ida Mae, however, relished all the attention—and then some—that had come from their reported encounter with the aliens.

To the point that the two of them had agreed to tell their stories, for a price, to one of the national tabloids. (Lucille had been approached by journalists from the same Florida-based tabloid, The National Enquirer, and had resolutely declined to share anything with them.)

Why muddy the waters even further, she reasoned, *by agreeing to talk to such a sleazy publication?*

Yes, she could use the generous money that would go along with her agreeing to talk, but what about her reputation—or at least what was left of it?

For already, Lucille was getting the cold shoulder from some of her close friends and acquaintances at church.

Since shortly after what she had described to police as "the abduction," no one sat on the same pew with her.

The women she had gotten close to in the prayer shawl ministry at church weren't as eager to share any kind of news with her or include her in special projects.

People, a few of them whispering to one another, also kept their distance when they encountered Lucille in a store or restaurant.

It wasn't that they had become her enemies. It was more like they had become cold, detached, not wishing to be associated with a woman who, to some folks' way of thinking, had cooked up the biggest tall tale in the history of Horry County, South Carolina.

One deacon at her church wasn't convinced Lucille had been deceitful.

"Why would a fine woman who's never told a lie in her whole life just flat out invent something so strange and bizarre and file a police report about it?" the deacon asked. "What would she have to gain by lying?"

"You tell me," a skeptic shot back. "And you might start by asking how much her two close friends—Maxine Robinson and Ida Mae James—are getting paid for telling their story to the National Enquirer. "And not only that, I hear tell that the two of 'em's going on the speaking circuit. You know what I mean—all them meetings and conventions and such that those folks who believe in flying saucers go to. There must be big money in that stuff."

The deacon responded: "I hear what you're sayin' but Lucille Mulligan is different. I'm tellin' you, she's a straight arrow. Never told a fib in her life and she's not tryin' to make money off any of this. Matter of fact, she's quit talking, period, about what happened that night that she came into contact with the flying saucer or whatever it was. She can't help what Maxine and Ida Mae's doin'. That's not Lucille and never will be. She's just not made that way. She's an upstanding Christian woman and what she says is the God's honest truth."

"So you say," said the skeptic, grinning. "So you say. When the jingle of the guinea's involved, anything's possible. Anything at all, my man."

The deacon stood his ground:

"Lucille Mulligan just wants to be left alone. She wants to live the rest of her days in peace and not be tormented about what lots of folk're sayin' about her. Believe me, she's a good woman. And I know she's not a liar. She can't help it if people doubt her."

Chapter 8
We Know What We Are

As borderline reclusive and mum as Lucille Mulligan was, her two close friends, Maxine Robinson and Ida Mae James, couldn't have been more talkative.

They had spoken freely to any and all people who'd asked them about their experience with what had become known as their "flying saucer encounter."

And Maxine, especially, had actively sought out opportunities to cash in on it.

"Well, why the devil shouldn't we get paid for what we went through?" Maxine told Ida Mae. "Wouldn't anybody else do the same thing if they was in our shoes?"

At first, Ida Mae wasn't so sure.

Because already she'd heard murmurings that the three women had made the whole thing up just to get attention.

None of that swayed Maxine, however.

"Well, let 'em think and guess and gossip all they want," she said. "The fact is, it happened and we won't ever be the same so we might as well make the most of it."

True enough, Ida Mae conceded, but still, something about trying to collect money from such a strange, once-in-a-lifetime experience didn't seem right.

Which made Maxine all the more adamant.

She took hold of her friend's hands, locked eyes with her and said, "We know what we are, Ida Mae. We're just two, single, middle-aged women who are strugglin' day in and day out to make ends meet. And we happen to live in a place they call a little piece a paradise.

"But you know what we really are? We, and them like us down here at Myrtle Beach, are nothing but maids. You might even call us slaves or servants. All these rich folks—with their jewelry and Cadillacs and BMWs—move down here from New York or New Jersey. And you know who takes care of 'em, who washes their clothes, cleans their big fine houses, trims their trees, mows their yards, cleans their hotel rooms, and cooks and serves their meals in our restaurants?

"It ain't, for sure, all them New York retirees," Maxine said. "It's us. We know who and what we are, Ida Mae. We're here to fetch and tote and scrub toilets and work our you-know-whats off just for their benefit. So ain't it about time the shoe got on the other foot? Don't we deserve a little piece a pie?"

Maxine ended her plea with asking her friend when the last time was she'd been on an ocean cruise to, say, the Dominican Republic or the Caymans or St. John or Aruba.

Ida Mae, dropping her head, said she didn't even know where those places were.

"That's exactly my point, dear! You and I are due to live a little. And maybe that's why this whole thing happened us. You ever thought about it like that? I want what them New York broads have. I want their diamonds and their cruise ship vacations and their country club memberships.

"And I might even run up on me a man before this is over," she said slyly.

Ida Mae noted that Lucille Mulligan was keeping to herself and not talking to anyone. "So how," she asked, "was it fair that we'd profit financially and not her?"

"Because you're talking about Lucille," Maxine said. "And Lucille does what Lucille wants to do and nobody will ever convince her otherwise. If she wants to stay at home with her damn spoiled dog and birds and plants—and not travel or have some of the finer things in life—that's her call. But you and me, we're different.

"Think of it this way, Ida Mae. How much more time do we have left on this planet to do what we really wanna do or go where we wanna go? We ain't gettin' a day younger!"

Ida Mae hugged her friend tightly and whispered in her left ear, "So, where do we start?"

"By promisin' me you won't chicken out with me on talkin' to that reporter from the National Enquirer."

"But what if he asks me something I can't answer or don't remember?" Ida Mae interjected.

"Let me handle that, Ida Mae. I'll be right there with you. We'll insist that he interview us together. So if you get nervous or can't find your words or whatever, I'll fill in the gaps. And the more far-fetched or unbelievable something seems, the better. Not that we need ta be makin' anything up. I ain't sayin' that at all. Cause what happened ta us'll speak for itself. That's how they sell their magazine or newspaper or whatever you want to call it.

"You know what Adolph Hitler said? He said that the bigger the lie, the more people will believe it."

Ida Mae asked Maxine if she really thought the National Enquirer would pay them $5,000 for their story.

"Nope. We're going to ask for double that," Maxine said. "And they'll be lucky if we don't ask for even triple what they're offerin'. Because the public wants to know about this in the worst way. Cain't hardly stand to wait a day longer."

Ida Mae's eyes seemed to get bigger, her pulse quickened, and her demeanor grew more excited as her friend continued talking.

She asked her how much it cost to take a cruise to an island where it was always warm and sunny and you could get pedicures and massages to your heart's delight.

"Don't make no difference, Ida Mae, cause this'll be just the beginning. You an' I're goin' on a lotta trips out west."

Ida Mae asked, "Out west? Why out west?"

"Because that's where most folks say they've seen these flying saucers, and some even swear to God to bein' taken up in 'em."

"So you believe 'em?"

Maxine acted annoyed.

"I really don't know and I don't care! And what in tarnation difference does it make? I only know that we're ready for some excitement and money. Now are you with me or not?"

Ida Mae nodded yes and started giggling.

"I've always wanted to go to Las Vegas. Have any flyin' saucers landed there? Think we'd be invited there?"

"I'd say the odds are pretty good, dear. Because how far could it be from Roswell, New Mexico, to Las Vegas? And I'm sure we'll get booked in Roswell."

"Whadya mean, Roswell?" Ida Mae asked. "Why would we be goin' there?"

Tempted to lash out at Ida Mae for her naïveté, Maxine instead controlled herself and calmly educated her friend.

"Because, dear, if you know anything at all about UFO's, you know that Roswell, New Mexico, is where the aliens landed on this planet in 1947."

Still looking dumbfounded, Ida Mae asked her to explain.

"What's there to explain, dear? Everybody knows about Roswell. There's been books written about it. Movies made about it. TV shows. You name it. You might say that Roswell started the whole thing when it came to flyin' saucers."

Ida Mae wondered out loud if solid proof existed for the existence of aliens.

"Of course we have solid proof," Maxine said emphatically. "A sheepherder on a ranch outside Roswell said he'd found where a flyin' saucer had crashed in his pasture, and then one a' his neighbors said she saw the government transportin' the dead aliens in an ambulance.

"And wouldn't ya know it? Not so much as a trace ever turned up of those two corpses. And our great big all powerful federal government never would say a thing about what happened to the UFO wreckage or to them bodies.

"But every year in Roswell, folks still gather ta mark the anniversary of that UFO sightin' there all them years ago.

"And ya know how they do it? They have all kinds 'a festivals in Roswell, and they dress us like aliens and have dance and costume contests, and they have experts come from the Air Force or Navy or what have you and talk about tha' latest UFO sightings. They give presentations and show pictures of UFOs and folks hang on ever' word they say.

"And that's why you and me'd be goin' to Roswell, New Mexico. To be among believers and ta tell 'em, in our own words, our story."

When Ida Mae asked her how they could possibly afford to go to such a faraway place, Maxine assured her that all their expenses—airfare, hotel, food and entertainment—would be covered.

"Ya see, Ida Mae, all these flyin' saucer groups have dues their members have ta pay, and I'm sure they use part'a that money to bring people like us to their get togethers.

"So we'll be helpin' them, and they'll be helpin' us. It's like a two-way street. We've got somethin' they want to hear from us, and they've gotta good bit'a money to spend just to bring folks like us to their meetin's. It's win-win for everybody."

Chapter 9
Keeping The Skies Safe

With a reluctant thumbs up from my boss, as he put it, to "turn over some rocks and see what you can find out about this damned flying saucer crap," I decided to pay a visit to the powers that be at Myrtle Beach International Airport.

Specifically, for my purposes, that would be none other than Ted Staley, head man in the 80-year-old airport's air traffic control tower.

I had never met Staley but had first heard his name from the local TV news reports a few days earlier. Channel 23, the CBS affiliate, had tantalized its viewers, saying the station had learned from Staley that, yes, something, odd had been detected by the airport's radar.

So odd that Staley had sent an electronic copy of the radar report to the commander of the jet fighter squadron at Charleston Air Force Base.

But not so unusual, at the time the blips appeared on the radar screen, that Staley had seen fit to ask that the Air Force scramble fighter jets to get a visual I.D.

But Staley, according to the latest Channel 23 news report, had supposedly been re-thinking his no-scramble decision.

No doubt, although I didn't have evidence to prove this, he'd gotten heat from the public about his initial thinking.

I had been reading some of the Facebook posts about this—many of them mentioning what happened when the Japanese invaded Pearl Harbor in 1941.

The U.S military had just installed radar at that time on Hawaii. No one, it seemed, really had a good handle on how powerful it was or how exactly it worked, but radar blips had appeared on the Army's radar screen that early morning of December 7 all those years ago.

Lowly ranked enlisted soldiers monitoring the screens, known as "scope dopes" in Air Force lingo today, were alarmed and immediately reported the strange, unexpected blips to their superior in Hawaii.

The rest is history. The commander discounted the blips as merely friendly incoming U.S. aircraft that had neglected to file flight plans.

Minutes later, invading Japanese aircraft bombed or strafed U.S. Navy warships and destroyed other key U.S. military armament.

Hawaii went up in flames and thousands died, thanks to a bad decision by a young Army second lieutenant who had discounted the radar blips.

It seemed no such tragedy, or anything remotely like it, was about to happen in Myrtle Beach in 2021 under the watch of Ted Staley.

Local TV news journalists, however, had failed to follow up Staley's reported assertion that he was re-thinking his decision about the Air Force jets.

That was typical ratings driven broadcast journalism, I thought. *Being the first on the scene with a report, whetting the public's appetite with some of the more curious details, and promising to follow-up. And then dropping the ball or forgetting about the story altogether.*

I waited in a holding area near the elevator beneath the airport tower. My interview with

Staley was scheduled in 15 minutes, and he had told me by email he was allotting me half an hour.

Not a lot of time but enough to find out, I hoped, what his current thinking was. Had he changed his mind about not asking the Air Force to investigate the reported flying objects off the coast of Surfside Beach?

I got a text tone that he was ready to see me.

The interview started on a less than promising note.

"I've already spoken publicly on what I know about what happened that day," Staley said, his body language betraying a reluctance to say anything more. "So I don't see what else I can add. But I know you media folks'll milk this for all its worth."

I thanked him again for talking to me and then got directly to the point.

"It's been said that you're maybe having second thoughts about not asking the Air Force to scramble their jets that day. Is that the case."

He cleared his throat, folded his arms in front of him, and showed a hint of a slight smile.

"Well, let's put it this way. A lot of people in Myrtle Beach now say they're afraid because of what I DIDN'T DO. And there's this talk of a coverup on my part which is absolutely absurd. If I were to pick up that red phone right now," he said, pointing to a phone just a few feet from where we sat in the computer-screen circled aircraft control tower, "General Roger Danner or his next in command would answer it on the first ring.

"Do you know who he is?" Staley, grinning slyly, asked.

When I said that I didn't and tried to stay focused on what he was saying to me—amid all the crackling radio static and hectic, busyness of the about 10 employees in the aircraft control tower—he eagerly enlightened me.

"He happens to be the commander of the 118th Fighter Squadron at Charleston Air Force Base. And he and I go way back—to my days when I myself was an Air Force pilot."

"Thank you for your service, Sir."

Staley ignored that comment and went on to explain to me that F-16C Falcon fighter combat jets were at the ready, 24 hours a day, seven days a week, and could be airborne from Charleston in 5-10 minutes.

"All I have to do is say SCRAMBLE!" he said, and those jets'll be at Myrtle Beach in hardly any time at all.

"And might I also note that they're armed with lethal missiles.

"I'm telling you all this to let you know that I am well aware of the consequences of what happens if and when I give the SCRAMBLE directive to my good friend, the general, in Charleston."

"But why didn't you, sir, ask them to scramble, given that you didn't know what those radar blips were that day?" I asked politely but firmly. "Isn't that part of your responsibility—keeping our skies safe around Myrtle Beach?"

"BECAUSE, YOUNG MAN, IT WOULD MEAN I'D LATER HAVE TO FILE A TON OF MINDLESS PAPERWORK JUSTIFYING MY DECISION! AND ALL FOR WHAT, EXACTLY? A BUNCH OF SEAGULLS OR CANADIAN GEESE FLYING IN FORMATION?!"

Staley's face reddened and I noticed his jaws tightening.

"I don't for one second like what you are implying—that I didn't do my job. And I've had quite enough of this interview already. So if you're done..."

"So you didn't ask the jets to scramble cause you'd have to fill out some forms? Is that about it in a nutshell?

"The way you say that is almost insulting," he snapped.

"Young man, do you see that runway out there? It's almost two miles long and we service nine major airlines, many of them flying to more than 50 destinations nonstop.

"Myself and my extremely devoted employees in this tower make sure day in and day out that all those aircraft arrive and depart smoothly and safely. Tens of thousands of passengers rely on us daily.

"We do everything in our power to keep our skies and our grounds safe. We are in touch with the pilots of those aircraft almost every minute—keeping them informed about the weather, about altitude and winds and speed, and we even help them taxi to the terminal."

I could hear the steady hum of aircraft control chatter as Staley went on with his diatribe.

"I can see, sir, that you're a very busy man, as is your crew," I said, extending my hand and thanking him again for his time.

"I just have one more question. If I need anything else from you, may I feel free to call you? Can I have your cell number."

"No and no," he said pointedly. "I'm sure you can find your way out."

With that, he walked away and I did an about face and headed toward the elevator just a few feet away.

But as I stood there waiting for the doors to open, a young woman, whose nametag said INTERN, tapped me on the shoulder. She glanced around quickly, then put a piece of paper in my hand.

I opened it in the elevator. It had her name and cell number and the request, "Call me. It's important."

Chapter 10
The Truth Hurts

Fresh back from the airport to the newsroom of the Ocean Herald, editor Charles Wallace spotted me and signaled for me to meet him in his office.

"So what's the skinny?" he asked, stretching out and yawning behind his desk.

"About what?"

"You know damned well what I'm talking about. Whadya find out from Mr. Bigshot in the air traffic control tower?"

I told him exactly what I'd learned from Ted Staley.

That being that he decided not to ask the Air Force to scramble jets that day because of all the burdensome paperwork he'd have to fill out.

"So, doesn't sound like you have much of a story, Lester. All you've got, it seems to me, is a couple of beer drinkin' fishermen at the beach saying they saw somethin' odd in the sky. Some sorta objects that coulda been anything—weather balloons, drones, flares. Who really knows what they saw? And we're supposed to cover it?"

"Sir, with all due respect, it was more than Mr. and Mrs. Gray swearing they saw the flying objects. Dozens of other people at Surfside Beach have corroborated their story."

"And how do you know they haven't all gotten together and cooked this whole farfetched thing up—just to embarrass the likes of gullible folks like you, Lester? And to get their names in the paper. They're probably already laughing at us behind our back."

I told him I thought that was highly unlikely. Then I reminded Wallace about the three local women—Lucille Mulligan, Maxine Robinson, and Ida Mae James—who'd taken a lie detector test and subjected themselves to hypnosis.

I reminded him that such procedures, conducted by state appointed experts, supported the idea that the women had told the truth.

"So you're sayin' that you believe those three fruitcakes actually had their car stopped by aliens in a UFO?"

"I'm just saying, sir, that we report what people say. That's our job as journalists. Then let our readers decide for themselves what's fact versus fiction.

"The truth emerges from many voices, Sir."

"No need to lecture me about the basics of journalism, young man because I've been doing this for longer than you've been on this earth!

"Now, I believe, if I'm not mistaken, that you've got a story to write about your conversation with Mr. Ted Staley. So get to it!

"By the way, I've spoken to that guy before and he strikes me as somewhat of a pompous ass. Let's you know, soon as you meet him, that he's a mister biggety big at the airport. He didn't impress me in the least."

I returned to my desk, looked over my notes from my interview with Staley, and decided to call him to ask if he wanted to add anything to our conversation.

Just as I expected, both of my calls, 30 minutes apart, went unanswered to his voicemail.

Next, I reached out to General Roger Danner, commander of the fighter jet squadron at Charleston Air Force Base.

Surprisingly, I got right through to his administrative assistant, an Air Force staff sergeant, and then to the general himself.

The man in charge of the combat-ready F-16C jets at Charleston—the mainstay of the Air Force's aerial war fleet—couldn't have been more open and accommodating.

"Why yes, I've known air traffic control director Staley for many years, and when that airport up at Myrtle Beach was an Air Force base, I flew jets out of there myself. Quite a nifty runway y'all have up there, and Ted and his crew do a bang-up job of organizing all those arrivals and departures. Not an easy thing when your airport has only one runway."

I asked him what would have happened a few days ago had Staley requested him to scramble his jets.

"They woulda been there practically faster than you coulda said unidentified flyin' object," the general quipped. "Because it doesn't take long to go 98 miles when you're ridin' in a 20-million-dollar jet that can go twice the speed of sound."

Then I asked him about a worst-case scenario: if the objects off the coast of Surfside Beach were deemed to be a threat, who would give the order to shoot them down.

"That would come from the senior director on duty at NORAD—which is the North American Air Defense Command. If he gives me the green light, I instruct my pilots to fire their missiles.

"But I hope it never comes to that, of course. And so do my pilots. We're here to protect and defend. We like to think of ourselves as a deterrent. We'd only go on offense as a last resort."

As to Staley's decision not to scramble, the general said that wasn't his call to second guess.

Lastly, I brought up the topic of unidentified flying phenomena—the umbrella term the U.S. government now uses to cover UFOs.

"I really wouldn't have any comment on that, other than to say, I guess, that the jury is still out on such phenomena," the general said, choosing his words carefully.

General Danner added: "I've heard about the reports coming out of Myrtle Beach, and I'd be the last to dismiss them as out of hand, but neither am I joining the party. I do know this. Sometimes a person wants to believe something so badly that that skewers their judgment. And they see or hear things that are, pardon the pun, out of this world. Not, mind you, that I'm casting all such people as delusional or liars, but give me some hard, incontrovertible evidence. Something I can take to the bank. Then I'll maybe become a believer."

Confident that I had enough to write at least a brief account of I had learned, I tapped out a few hundred words that were immediately posted online. My story also was set to appear in tomorrow's print edition of the Ocean Herald:

```
By Lester Harmless
General Assignment Reporter
The Ocean Herald

The man in charge of air traffic
control at Myrtle Beach International
Airport explained this week why he
didn't order Air Force jets to scramble
to identify the unidentified flying
```

objects reported a few days ago off the coast of Surfside Beach.

Air traffic control director Ted Staley said he declined to give the scramble order because of what he described as burdensome paperwork that he'd have to fill out.

He acknowledged that airport radar had detected blips that day, indicating two unidentified airborne objects in the sky at Surfside Beach but noted that asking Air Force jets to scramble out of Charleston would have involved "mindless" paperwork. It would have also taken valuable time away from his primary mission of ensuring the safe arrivals and departures of aircraft at Myrtle Beach International Airport.

Had Staley contacted the commander of the 118th Fighter Squadron at Charleston Air Force Base and asked him to scramble and dispatch supersonic jets to the sky at Surfside Beach, those jets would have been airborne within 5 minutes and on the scene within just a few minutes later.

That's according to General Roger Danner, commander of the fighter squadron. Danner said that the actual order to shoot down any unknown aerial objects would have to come from NORAD, which is the nuclear bomb-proof air defense headquarters for North America located under Cheyenne Mountain in Colorado.

Two unknown circular orange objects in the sky—described by witnesses as "big as houses"—were reportedly seen just off the coast of Surfside Beach earlier this week.

Barry Gray and his wife Becky had been fishing at Surfside Beach when they reported witnessing the mysterious airborne objects darting back and forth at hypersonic speed.

Dozens of others at the beach also said they saw the same thing, with more than one witness vowing that they'd seen bonafide unidentified flying objects (UFOs).

A few, who didn't want to speak on the record, went as far as to describe what they saw as "other worldly" or as proof of alien presence at Myrtle Beach.

Meanwhile, two weeks ago, three local women—Lucille Mulligan, Maxine Robinson, and Ida Mae James—said the vehicle they'd been riding in had been stopped by a mysterious huge disc-shaped flying object. The women have sworn, and their stories have been corroborated by polygraph tests and a hypnotist, that they were beamed up into the object and examined, but not harmed, by strange difficult-to-describe creatures.

97

More will be published on these stories
as information becomes available.

The print story appeared the next day in the newspaper—below the fold on page 2. With the headline:

Director of Air Traffic Control at Airport Declines to Request Scramble of Air Force Jets

The secondary deck headline was:

Acknowledges Airport Radar Detecting Unknown Aerial Objects But Says He Didn't Want To Be Bothered With 'Mindless" Paperwork

Appearing alongside my story was a photo—from our files—of Ted Staley accepting the Grand Strand Man of the Year award last year from the Myrtle Beach Chamber of Commerce. The caption under the picture read that Staley had been honored for his "countless years of selfless, diligent hard work in aviation on behalf of all persons living on the Grand Strand."

The photo showed a smiling Staley accepting a commemorative plaque from the chamber president. They were shaking hands and the

98

president, with his other hand was pointing at Staley akin to how a basketball player points at a teammate who's just made a great assist.

In the background were Staley's wife and their three children, all beaming with pride.

In journalism parlance, it was the typical grip and grin photo.

Shortly after the paper came out, I was summoned posthaste to editor Wallace's office.

There with him, again, was the introverted (to put it mildly) executive editor and the publisher.

Wallace told me to close the door and take a seat.

"It looks like, Lester, that you've stirred up a bit of a hornet's nest because me and my esteemed colleagues here have been getting calls all morning.

"And, as you know when people contact the newspaper, they usually have a fish to fry.

"And this is no different, Lester."

Wallace went on to explain that they had fielded threatening calls from Staley and his family members, as well as from the executive director of the Chamber of Commerce.

All were demanding a retraction and sincere apology from the paper.

"A retraction for what specifically, exactly?" I asked nervously.

"That's just it, young man. They're not clear on what they're wanting us to correct," publisher Huntington chimed in. "But they all agree on one thing: your story makes Ted Staley look like an unmitigated, self-centered idiot."

Editor Wallace, I could tell, was trying hard to suppress a chuckle.

No one said anything for a few seconds.

And then the publisher spoke.

"I think, under the circumstances, that this is a sensitive story that we should stay on top of, regardless of what kind of pressure we get. So I applaud you, Charles and Lester, for your work on this so far. Please stay the course. As I always say, just tell the truth and be fair. That's all I ask."

"And if I may, Ma'am, I always say something similar," Wallace said. "What we're supposed to be doing around here is telling the truth and raisin' hell!"

With that, everyone rose from their chairs and took turns shaking my hand. That is, with the exception of the executive editor, who hadn't spoken a word and was likely focused on returning to the putting green in his office.

Wallace even gave me a pat on the back after the other two had exited, adding: "I still think all this flyin' saucer stuff is a load of you know what, but you know what? It riles people up and sells papers.

"So go for it, Lester. But be careful. As I always say, keep the swamps drained so you can see the alligators. Because this is one of those stories that can come back in a heartbeat and bite you on the ass."

"Yes, Sir."

Chapter 11
Surprise Visitor

The old man, now in his early 80s, sat in what he called his "man cave" in his garage.

He lived at the end of a lonely tree-lined cul-de-sac in a gated upper middle-class Myrtle Beach community just a few miles from the ocean.

Three out of every four homes there were occupied by "damn Yankee northerners," as their southern counterparts called them.

They were mostly deep-pocketed New York or New Jersey retirees who'd moved south, like so many of their ilk, to escape high taxes and brutal weather.

Where they lived now had lush Bermuda grass lawns, palm trees, and crepe myrtles. Their homes were all about the same size but yet different— with a few split levels scattered among the sleek ranches.

It was one of those cozy subdivisions where retired well-heeled Northerners took good care of their property—or rather hired Mexicans or locals to do it for them. A golf cart's ride from the beach, residents enjoyed walking or lazing at the HOA pool. They also frequently called their friends and family in the cold, snowy north and boasted about how nice it was at the beach.

The man in his garage man cave was Phillip Roscoe Brown, but to those who knew him he was just plain old "Roscoe"—a widowed grandfather who'd moved south from Delaware years ago to go saltwater fishing, boating and golfing.

His days of catching fish and swinging his golf clubs behind him, about the only thing he now did was take care of his disabled sister, sit in his man cave, and tend to his lawn.

And who, really, could blame him?

What with his partially paralyzed sister growing more frail by the month, this is what he did to pass the time.

While she slept, or read books on her iPad, he held vigil in his man cave. With the garage door always wide open so he didn't miss anything. He had his favorite place well equipped, with a high-speed internet-connected computer, a remote camera so he could keep a close watch on his sister, his cell phone, coffee maker, and micro fridge.

A good day was when he spotted a shapely woman in shorts walking her dog.

An exceptionally good one was when that same woman would mosey up to him and chat.

Not that he had much in the way of carnal desires. For he hadn't felt even a twinge of such in years.

But an old fellow could still look. After all, no harm in looking at the menu as long as you didn't eat the food.

On a dull day, when no one was out walking, the old man fetched his powerful hunter's slingshot. He kept it ready to fire within an arm's length of where he sat.

It was his tool of choice for killing squirrels. Or for shooing away the flocks of Canadian geese that occasionally wandered into his yard.

Because, after all, who liked to step into a pile of goose poop?

Larry C. Timbs Jr.

And who could put up with rat-like squirrels gnawing their way into your attic?

On this particular day, however, it wasn't a dog-walking woman who stopped by to talk.

Rather, it was a male acquaintance who lived a couple of blocks away. He'd just lost his wife to a car accident.

He was in his late 60s, and though Roscoe didn't know him very well, the distraught looking man obviously wanted someone to talk to.

Over six feet tall and with graying sideburns and a neatly trimmed goatee, he had a receding hairline and a furrowed forehead. He carried a walking stick—likely not so much to lean on but to scare off any aggressive dogs.

He soon learned that both the man and his wife had been injured in the car collision. However, the man had been saved by his seatbelt. His unstrapped wife had taken the brunt of the collision and had not survived.

Choking back tears, the man said, "I survived because I kept eating and walking and getting on with my life, but Linda didn't because she wouldn't get out of bed or go to physical therapy. I just couldn't make her get up. And then she came down with pneumonia."

Roscoe, not knowing exactly how to respond, came up with: "It was probably meant to be. No need to blame yourself."

But the suffering soul insisted that if he'd dragged his wife out of the bed, she'd still be breathing.

"You don't know that," said Roscoe consolingly. "You did the best you could, and you yourself survived. So now you've got to live in the present."

Rising suddenly from his perch and trying to change the subject, Roscoe yelled, "Just look at those damn squirrels! Ain't they the most brazen little varmints you ever saw? They eat up all my bird feed. Then they gnaw their way into my attic and make a mess up there and ramble around at all hours of the day and night. Nothing but pests!"

His mission in life the past few years: keep the squirrels and geese out of his yard.

But the man didn't seem interested.

He continued grieving for his wife and blaming himself for her death.

So Roscoe just kept listening, not knowing quite what else to say.

"You know, Linda and I used to ride past that cemetery on Miller Ridge Parkway. Pleasant Grove Cemetery is the name of it," the man said. "And I remember one day she said to me, 'Wouldn't that be a beautiful place to be buried? It's so peaceful and lovely.'

"She was just talking off the top of her head, never imaginin' in a thousand years that within a few weeks that's exactly where she'd end up.

"And that's where I put her. They're making a marker for her now. And you know, the weird thing is it'll have both her name and my name on it. With the year I was born but they'll have to wait till you know when to put..."

The man's voice trailed off.

He apologized for taking up so much of Roscoe's time.

But Roscoe, good listener that he was, said he understood completely, and that if he ever needed to talk again, he was all ears.

But no sooner had the man taken 20 steps did he turn around and ask Roscoe if he'd seen anything strange in the sky lately.

"Something's goin' on that I can't explain," the man said. "And I guess you've been keepin' up with the news of those UFOs?"

Roscoe didn't subscribe to the Ocean Herald or to any other printed newspaper. He was like most folks these days, preferring to get his news via his smart phone. But he said he'd caught the tail end of a recent TV newscast—something about big orange disc shaped flying objects spotted over the ocean at Surfside Beach.

"So whadya make of it all?" the man asked him. "Because personally I think we're in the End Times. Meanin' it ain't gonna' make no difference what any of us try to do. Them that's not killed by criminals or accidents or diseases'll be taken up into the clouds by Jesus.

"And my dear Linda'll come out of her grave.

"So are you a Christian, Roscoe? Do you believe in the Second Coming of Christ. I have a feelin' that those UFOs have somethin' to do with Jesus coming back."

Roscoe, who hadn't darkened a church door in many years, nevertheless said no one knew when Jesus was returning to earth.

"But do I believe he's comin'. You're damn right. As sure as geese are poopin' on my yard, and as sure as the squirrels are rummagin' in my bird feeders. Yeah, he's comin' back.

"But do I think it has one frickin' thing to do with those flying saucers, or whatever strangeness it was those folks say they saw in the sky? Now that, my good man, is a God-damned open question."

"Ya know, Roscoe, something IS about to happen," the man said. "I feel it in my bones. I can't rightly explain it, but somehow, when I lost my Linda I had a sense it really didn't matter anymore who died. We look up into the sky and see things that blow our mind. No one knows what's going on."

"So you're saying, my friend, that those things people swear they've seen are from another planet?" Roscoe said. "And they're being flown not by human beings but by little green aliens? Again, show me the proof."

Roscoe fetched a cold beer from his microfridge, popped the top, and offered it to his visitor. But the man declined it.

Instead, he asserted that some things—and perhaps the most important things in life—you had to take by faith or feeling alone. Things like love, trust, and belief in a higher power.

Roscoe, who'd heard quite enough speculation about interstellar aliens and their spacecraft, wished him well and gave him a thumbs-up wave good-bye.

With that, the man walked off.

And Roscoe, as he did every day until a bit after sunset, remained ensconced in his garage man cave. Near dark, he'd put the garage door down, turn off his computer, and get ready for bed. But not before checking to see that his sister had everything she needed to get through another night.

* * *

A little after midnight that same evening, all was quiet a few miles away at the sprawling Pleasant Grove Cemetery. Giant pine trees formed a border separating the cemetery from adjoining wetland. A cloudy, surreal-like mist descended on the tombstones. Listen carefully and you could hear the hoot of an owl. A coyote howled in a nearby swamp. Gators, turtles, raccoons, and water moccasins scavenged for food.

At the still-yet unmarked grave of Linda Sue Dickinson of Myrtle Beach, South Carolina—one of thousands of Americans who'd died on the highway—it was, like the rest of the cemetery, cool, quiet, peaceful, and lonely.

Because, after all, who goes to a cemetery, a place of death and mourning and painful losses—at midnight?

On this night, however, an intense beam of light lit up Linda's gravesite.

The origin of that powerful light: a huge circular spacecraft that had traveled millions of miles, light years if you will, from another star to earth.

Tonight, the bizarre looking craft just hovered. It made no sound, and whatever or whoever was in it seemed content to merely hang there in the air and illuminate the grave site. As it did that, a thick, heavy fog seemed to emanate from beneath the enormous spacecraft and onto the gravesite. Because of the fog, had you been looking, you wouldn't have been able to see the exact spot where Mrs. Dickinson had been laid to rest.

And you would have thought it extremely unlikely, because of the out-of-the-way location and late hour, that anyone witnessed any of this.

And then, as soundlessly and quickly as the spacecraft had appeared, its lights blinking, it was gone.

Faster and more powerful and more beautiful than anything humans had ever built.

Or could even imagine building.

Because this "craft"—regardless of where it came from or who or what created and controlled it— instantly accelerated and shot across the night sky faster than a bullet.

Had someone noticed, they might have mistaken it for a shooting star or meteor.

Chapter 12
Academic Help

Once the fuss from the Staley clan had fizzled, I turned my attention to Dr. Henry Evans, the astronomy professor at Coastal Carolina University.

Evans, at the tail end of my visit to his home, had mentioned that I should call him about the reported mysterious sighting in the sky. Maybe he could help me in my coverage—or words to that effect.

Nothing to lose, so I connected with him and he immediately brought up his son Justin, who apparently was doing well with his physical therapy. But he said the lawnmower accident injuries, especially those to Justin's face, neck, and upper torso would still take many more months to heal.

"It's a marathon for recovery for my son, not a race, as you know," the professor reminded me. "But Nora and I thank you so much for how you've handled reporting on Justin. And how you snapped his picture right before you left our home. That was a really nice gesture.

"Not that I ever thought you'd publish it, but just taking the picture made him happy."

We were sitting in his office in the astronomy department at the university. First thing I noticed, upon taking my seat, was a painting of a NASA rocket. It hung on a wall beside his cluttered desk next to another painting—this one apparently a sci-fi portrait of a large disc-shaped object hovering over a grove of trees. At the foot of the snow-covered trees, which could have been blue spruces, were two deer, one with antlers, staring upward at a beam of light projected from the object.

The artist's name, which I couldn't quite make out, appeared in black ink in the lower right corner.

"I see you've spotted my pride and joy—a painting of an extraterrestrial spacecraft that abducted three women in Kentucky in the late 1970s."

The professor stared at the painting as if he were seeing it for the first time. And he seemed pleased that it had caught my attention.

"I like to tell my students that this is my physical proof that aliens from another world have visited our planet. Because, after all, the person who painted that picture was one of the three taken aboard the UFO that night. When it happened, it was covered by statewide media and by the National Enquirer. At that point in time, it was the most famous UFO sighting in the history of Kentucky."

I asked him if the signature in the lower right corner of the portrait was that of one of the abductees. He confirmed that indeed it was.

"So what kind of reaction do you get from your classes?"

He said it ranged from outright disbelief and snickering to wondering if somehow the incident actually happened.

For him, the painting was priceless, because, as he put it, how many college professors in America owned a portrait of a UFO?

When I asked him how he came to possess it, he said that was a long story—best to be told at another time and place, perhaps over a few drinks.

"So, Dr. Evans, you said you might be able to help me with what's supposedly happening in the sky at the beach. How so?"

He said he'd get to that but he first asked me if I'd be interested in a walking tour of his department.

When I said I would, he promised to make it brief.

And so off we went.

I learned that the Department of Astronomy was housed within a part of the university that focused on physics and engineering.

He gave me a tour of two state-of-the-art Mac labs connected to one of the largest, most powerful telescopes in South Carolina. Located in a nearby separate building, called the Astronomy Observatory at Coastal Carolina University, the telescope's mirrors were said to be constructed of ultra-pure synthetic glass. The advanced $1 million, 36-inch diameter telescope enabled students, faculty and others to gaze into the heavens at objects up to thousands of light years from Earth.

"It used to be we could only see certain stuff in textbooks, but now, thanks to Big Chanty Eye—nickname for the telescope—we can take pictures or videos. Stars, planets, comets, asteroids. You name it. With Big Chanty, we can see and photograph it. All the celestial wonders of the cosmos are there for the viewing."

Further along in the tour, I saw students with soft drinks and backpacks huddled around tables in small study groups. I noticed their books were about physics, math, chemistry, planetary systems, cosmology, thermodynamics, electronics and engineering.

Some of them wore ragged or baggy clothes, with holes in the knees and pockets of their frayed jeans, and others were in their pajamas. Some had piercings in their nose, ears, or lips. A few had a mixture of blue and pink hair. All wore flip flops.

I couldn't help but think that some of these same students might be walking on Mars in the not-too-distant future. Or working on cutting edge technology for America's space program.

But, regardless of what covered their bodies, they all struck me as serious and focused on learning. I say that because many of them were studying note cards and highlighted passages in their textbooks.

117

A far cry from my journalism school days when most of us took the path of least resistance, doing just enough to get by and typically waiting till the last hour or minute to cram before a test.

"These kids really seem to be into astronomy," I remarked. "But where do they go when they get their degree?"

Dr. Evans told me the core mission of the department is to prepare astronomy majors for careers in science, engineering, or advanced technology.

I pressed him. "But where exactly will they end up working?"

He responded: "At NASA or the JPL, in the military, computer programming, aerospace engineering, telecommunications, and some'll go on from here to graduate school."

I said I was impressed.

Then I asked him about the department's four-year graduation rate, seeming to recall that where I went to college less than a third of the students earned their degrees within four years.

"Well, unfortunately, it's not as high as it should be, but we are increasingly under the gun from the central administration to get these kids out of here in four years. And that's not to even mention the pressure we're getting from the state department of education."

"But these kids seem really bright and committed," I said. "What's delaying them?"

Dr. Evans explained that college students these days take longer to graduate because many change their majors. And when you do that, it slows you down. Or students drop out of school and work and then drop back in. Or they purposefully linger on campus, not in a hurry at all to finish their coursework.

That last reason—the purposeful lingering—struck me as interesting. I asked him to clarify.

"Let's put it this way, Lester. Some of these kids think they've found manna when they're on our campus. And what, really, is there not to like? Free entertainment. Free food. Free housing. Beautiful environment. Smart, interesting people you can lean on or befriend."

I noted that nothing was free and that someone, their parents or a relative or the taxpayers in general, was footing the bill for those amenities.

"Doesn't matter to them, Lester. Many of 'em aren't paying a dime and that's all they care about. They're here and they're living the good life. And who, really, can blame them?"

I nudged the conversation toward the reason I was here.

He and I made our way back to his office, where he placed a notice on his door asking no one to disturb us. Then he closed the door and we both sat.

My eyes went back to the portrait of the UFO hanging on the wall. After all, how often is it that a person gets to see a picture of a flying saucer. And not only that, one painted by an actual witness who swore to being abducted by aliens.

"I guess I should start by telling you that I firmly believe in the existence of extraterrestrials," Dr. Evans said. "Not that I'm ashamed of that in any way whatsoever, but when you work in academia, you have to be careful of what you say and who you say it to."

"But you're a tenured professor," I said. "How can anyone hurt you for your speech? Last I heard, we all have a First Amendment right to freely express our beliefs and opinions."

Not so much if you're employed at a college or university, he assured me.

He explained that someone in his profession—a person you would least expect or be aware of—is always looking over your shoulder, parsing your every word, examining your emails, taking note of your conversations with colleagues and others, and asking around to see if you're pulling your weight or rocking the boat.

"We have freedom of speech around here, Lester, but I prefer to think of it as *pseudo* freedom of speech," he said. "As long as you are perceived as being a good citizen of the university, you are fine. Step out of line even one inch or ruffle any feathers—at the university or in the community— and there can be serious consequences.

"As in your teaching load can be increased. Or you can forget about getting that sabbatical you thought you'd earned. Or that promotion and pay increase you're long overdue for goes by the wayside.

"What I'm saying is this: The central administration of this university, as well as the state of South Carolina, which owns this institution, has, what shall we call them—incentives for their employees to toe the company line—24 hours a day, 7 days a week.

"And as for me, I like it around here. I like, for the most part, what I do, and I like my students. And as for my wife Nora—you've met her. She's very content here. Neither one of us has any desire to leave the beach.

"So all of what I've just said is to help put into meaningful context what I'm about to say next. That being, again, I firmly believe in the existence of extraterrestrial life. Matter of fact, I believe it so strongly that I've joined, under the table and off the record mind you, a number of professional organizations of like mindedness. Meaning these are groups that have one thing in common:

"That being that humanity is on the verge of discovering evidence of intelligent beings, lifeforms, creatures—whatever you want to call them—from a world we cannot even imagine."

I asked him how he could be so sure.

"Because the universe is awfully big, Lester. And we've found, just in the last few decades, hundreds of exoplanets—those being planets around stars. And most intriguing is that we believe that many of those exoplanets are similar to Earth—with water, oxygen, hydrogen, nitrogen, methane. All the ingredients necessary for life as we know it."

So if somebody or something alive is out there, I wondered aloud, why haven't they contacted us?

"That's the billion-dollar question," the professor replied. "Perhaps they're fearful of us and just want to keep their distance. Or maybe they have already reached out to us but in a way that we can't yet understand."

He paused for a few seconds and stared at the painting of the UFO on his wall.

"I believe firmly that in the not-to-distant future First Contact will be made. By that, I mean humanity will have proof positive of the existence of intelligent beings from another world.

"I say that in part because now we are beginning to have the technology—the telescopes, the satellites, the means of communication—to reach out to the far corners of the universe.

"It's just a matter of time till we find them or they find us. We are definitely not alone in this vast cosmos we call the universe, my good man."

I let all that sink in and then politely asked the man again how he thought he could help me.

He smiled, opened his office door slightly to make sure no one was nearby listening, and then closed it.

Then he looked me straight in the eye and lowered his voice.

"Let's put it this way, Lester. Think of me as your Deep Throat anonymous source on UFOs or extraterrestrials. If, in your reporting, you need a comment from an informed source—albeit an unnamed one—about aliens, feel free to call me on my cell. But promise me you'll not use my name. That's all I ask. I wouldn't want to alienate my colleagues here in the academy."

"Who very much don't believe in extraterrestrials from another world, right?" I asked.

"That's their public, skeptical posture, I'm afraid," the professor said. "And until undeniable evidence of First Contact is made, they will not change their mind.

"They very much prefer to be left alone in their little silos—teaching their classes, writing papers and books about arcane topics that hardly anyone will ever read, and serving as consultants from time to time for business or industry. The latter results in a nice bit of extra change in their pockets.

"What I'm saying is this: my colleagues here at the university, smug and comfortable, tend to avoid controversy or conflict at all costs. Their every word, action, and interaction is in the service of advancing their reputations, as well as the good name of their employer—this university. Anything coming their way that could rock the boat? They avoid it like the plague."

I responded: "So again, so much for freedom of thought and expression in our institutions of higher learning, correct?"

"Absolutely, undeniably correct," he said emphatically.

Chapter 13
Living The Good Life

Twenty-three hundred miles away from their homes in Myrtle Beach, Ida Mae James and Maxine Robinson lolled next to a giant outdoor pool on the rooftop of a luxury hotel.

They had booked separate rooms at the five-star resort on the strip in Las Vegas.

And before that, they'd flown first class, courtesy of the Mutual UFO Network (MUFON), a 50-year-old, 4,000-member nonprofit organization that has one core purpose: to find evidence of extraterrestrial life.

MUFON was paying for all their meals, round-trip air fare, and hotel accommodations.

And it was doing so gladly, eager to have the two women share their stories with hundreds of other believers who had made the trip to Vegas for the annual conference.

The two women from Myrtle Beach were advertised as keynote speakers—scheduled to address an audience of at least 2,000 people the next day.

Their presentations were to run for 45 minutes each. And each was to be followed by a 30-minute Q&A session from the audience.

It was all seeming a bit much for an increasingly nervous Ida Mae James.

Far as she could remember, the only time she had spoken to a group of people was when she gave a book report in junior high school. And those had been her classmates, not strangers, from all across the USA and even from abroad.

"What on earth WILL I say, Maxine?" she pleaded, as her friend, comfortably reclining next to her at the pool, sipped on a tall frosty Daiquiri.

In the pool immediately in front of the two women was an extremely tall, muscular, well-tanned man. He wore a gold necklace and had tattoos on both his arms. His glistening, coal black hair he had combed straight back, as if to keep from obstructing his face.

It struck Maxine that the water-treading fellow— who appeared to be in his mid-40s—was the incarnation of a Greek god.

"Would you just look at him, gal? Look at how his muscles practically stand up and tell ya that he means business. Isn't he the handsomest man you ever laid eyes on?"

Ida Mae, also nursing a Daiquiri, lowered her sunglasses and glanced at the man. She had to admit (to herself) that yes, he was quite the male specimen.

But her mind at the moment was on what she would say up on a stage in front of that massive audience.

After all, some one or some thing (Was it a group called MUFON? She wasn't exactly sure but Maxine had taken care of all the details.) had forked out a lot of money to bring the two women to Vegas.

"Ain't you the least bit worried, Maxine, about what we're gonna say tomorrow? I didn't sleep a'tall last night for worryin' 'bout it. Why, I'm sa nervous I'm tempted to catch a bus outta here tanite."

Maxine held up an index finger as if signifying to give her a moment, took another swallow of her drink, nibbled on a giant luscious strawberry, and adjusted her lounge chair.

Then she spoke firmly.

"We got here on a big fancy jet, and we're leavin' on a big fancy jet, Ida Mae. So I don't wanna hear no more foolish talk about takin' a bus outta here, for cryin' out loud.

"Because we are now officially, bonafide jet setters. That's exactly what we are. We don't take buses and we don't stay in cheap motels. All that's in our past. We're upper crust, Ida Mae.

"Don't ya get it? People are payin' good money to hear us talk. So I'm gonna' give 'em what they came for."

Ida Mae asked her good friend exactly what she planned to say.

"For one thing, I'm gonna tell 'em what we saw, when we saw it, and where. And I ain't sparin' no dee-tails. These folks're hungry for a good story about a flyin' saucer and I'm gonna give 'em one.

Time I get done with 'em, they'll be so excited, they'll pee their pants.

"But I'll save the best part for you, Ida Mae. I'll set the table, so to speak. You'll feed 'em the feast."

Maxine paused to let all this sink in. She stretched and yawned and took another sip of her poolside drink. She knew Ida Mae would question her and that she did—within seconds.

"So if you're coverin' the who, what, when, and where, what's that leave me? I'm s'posed ta talk for 40 minutes, but about what, exactly?"

Maxine told Ida Mae to put her drink down and listen to her closely.

"You're gonna tell 'em 'bout what them things did to us when they took us up inta their spaceship. Just keep it short 'n' simple and stick ta what ya know what they done ta us, Ida Mae."

"But I don't remember much, Maxine! And even if I did, there ain't much ta tell. They were dark, shadowy, weird. Hard ta describe—like nothin' I ever seen in my life. And then they put all three of us down on some kinda big table, and none of us could move. I DO REMEMBER THAT PART.

"And it was like I wuz in some kinda trance, with them starin' at me with their cold black eyes. And I wuz skeered ta death. I mean, who wouldn't be?!"

Maxine smiled and clasped Ida Mae's right hand. "That's exactly what you'll say when it's your turn to speak," she said reassuringly. "And the audience'll love it. They'll hang on your every word. Believe me, my dear, they won't be able to get enough of it."

"You're sure about that, Maxine? Even though I can't remember much and I might get nervous and start cryin' when I get to the part 'bout being laid out on that table or whatever it wuz."

Ida Mae looked at her friend hopefully, whose nod told her that she'd be okay.

"Just be yourself up there, Ida Mae," Maxine said. "That's what all these folks have come here for—to hear what we have ta say about that spaceship and the creatures that took us up into it in our own words."

Across the way from the pool, from within the casino hotel, Maxine and Ida Mae heard loud shouts of joy. The hotel management had relayed them throughout the premises via a public address system.

"You hear that, Ida Mae?! Someone just hit a jackpot! When we get back to our rooms and get dressed, we oughta hightail it to the casino. No tellin' what might happen!"

Not that the two of them knew diddly squat about gambling, but they had walked through the casino on their way to the pool.

They noticed a lot of people in their 70s, 80s, or 90s playing the slot machines. They were in their wheelchairs or walkers or propping themselves up with their canes. But they were nevertheless feeding the one-armed bandits with as many coins as they had, and as quickly as they could.

"You see that, Maxine?" Ida Mae had commented. "Why, them folks is spendin' their grandchildren's inheritances. I never seen such a thing!"

"They ain't doin' a thing wrong," Maxine had retorted. "After all, it's their own damned money and more power to 'em for enjoyin' what time they've got left in this world. Truth be known, those same selfish grandchildren's already got 'em put away in a nursin' home or they're about to. I say live ever' day like it's your last!"

The vibe of Las Vegas seemed to reflect that kind of thinking.

Everywhere Maxine and Ida Mae looked on the strip, they saw bejeweled, fur-clad women and men in tuxes with white jackets and sleek, expensive shoes.

Stretch limos, mostly containing Japanese tourists (or maybe they were Japanese business executives living in Vegas?) glided up and down the strip, stopping every now and then at a casino, hotel, or shop to pick up or unload passengers.

Dazzling lights and color-changing spectacular fountains seemed to scream that Vegas was like a place unlike anywhere else on the planet.

A lively, full of diamonds and gold and money glittering place that was made to spread your wings in and have fun like you could never have anywhere else.

If it involved sex, money, power, excitement, or beauty, you could find it in Vegas. All you wanted and then some. And, as the old saying went, what you did or said in Vegas stayed in Vegas.

Maxine thought of all this as she and Ida Mae ventured back to their room.

Yes, they had come to the ideal venue to share their story about the spaceship. And yes, of course, they were going to make the most of what had occurred that winter night a few weeks ago.

And why not? Maxine reasoned. *It was maybe why it had happened to us in the first place. Because nothing is really just the luck of the draw in this old world, is it?*

Chapter 14
Trouble At The Graveyard

Making my usual rounds of combing through the incident reports at the police department, one document jumped out at me.

It seemed that a grave digger at Pleasant Grove Cemetery, on the outskirts of Conway in Horry County, had noticed something highly unusual a couple of nights ago.

His name was Miles Elliott, but people knew the 65-year-old employee of a local funeral home as "Digger."

Quickly reading Digger's police report, I noticed a mention of a "UFO." That caused me to take a seat and read more closely.

The gist of it was that Mr. Elliott had completed a long, arduous day of digging graves at the cemetery and had decided to rest in his beat-up old van. He noted that he kept a bedroll and pillow in it and a few bites to eat just in case he couldn't, for whatever reason, make it home.

The "rest" in his van that particular instance turned into a nap, and the nap, helped along with his sleep-inducing meds and a pint of bourbon whiskey, graduated to a deep slumber.

So next thing he knew, Digger had passed out.

When he woke up, according to the police report, it was well past midnight. No one had apparently noticed him or his van. And so no one paid him any mind all those long hours as he slept.

Which wouldn't have been such a big deal had he been unconscious, say, in a shopping center parking lot or even on a side street in a residential area.

Because there are lots of vehicles parked there, at all hours of the day and night.

But not so in a cemetery.

I kept reading the police incident report and learned that within a few minutes of the grave digger waking up, he said he noticed something he'll never forget.

He described it as a "big orange flyin' somethin' like one a' them UFOs you hear 'bout in tha news."

What he saw had apparently lingered silently in one location—not more than 10-15 feet in the air above a particular gravesite.

He said he knew for certain that it was the final resting place of the late Linda Sue Dickinson because he himself, with the help of a backhoe and another worker with a shovel, had dug that grave earlier in the week.

The police incident report had my full attention. It went on to note that the so-called bright, orange-colored UFO hovered over the grave for a few minutes and then shot off soundlessly, quicker than a rocket, into the night.

Mr. Elliott had sensed that in some unexplainable way, the UFO had tampered with the grave above which it hung, maybe even somehow penetrating it.

"But that was hard to know for sure because of the dense fog that night," he said.

The report noted that Mrs. Dickinson's next of kin was a Mr. Randolph Dickinson of Surfside Beach.

And that was it. Nothing about whether the police were investigating. And no mention of whether the late Mrs. Dickinson's husband would be contacted. I asked the officer on duty for more information and he politely but firmly informed me that that was the absolute end of it, adding, "We've got a lot more better things to do than run down every Tom, Dick, and Harry's wild-ass claims about UFOs."

I thanked the officer just the same and left my card with him.

I left the police station and immediately did a web search for the phone number of Randolph Dickinson, not an easy task in these days of practically everyone having an unlisted cell phone number.

No success there so I turned to old reliable—Facebook.

And there his FB page was!

Along with his photo and part of the eulogy for his late wife, Linda Sue Dickinson. The couple, smiling and embracing one another in a picture, had just celebrated their 25th wedding anniversary when she died in an automobile accident.

I quickly learned that she had fought unsuccessfully to stay alive in the hospital and had been the love of her husband's life. She had also had a passionate commitment for service at her non-denominational church in nearby Murrell's Inlet. No children or survivors, except for her husband, Randolph, and the couple's beloved dog, Doodles.

I messaged Randolph Dickinson via the Facebook tool, telling him I was very sorry he'd lost his wife and that I'd very much like to speak with him. It had to do, I said, with a project I was working on at the newspaper.

Less than two hours later, he called me, curious about why I wanted to speak to him.

I decided to be completely open and honest with him.

I was, I told him, investigating the reported sightings of UFOs in our area and I had noticed a police report filed by a Mr. Miles Elliott, a grave digger at Pleasant Grove Cemetery.

"And so, what on earth has that got to do with my wife?" he asked incredulously.

I gave him a chance to calm down and said, "It relates to your wife, Sir, because Mr. Elliott told the police that he saw what he described as a UFO. He said it was hovering above your wife's gravesite a couple of nights ago."

That got his attention, big time.

"Would you repeat that, please? I'm not sure I heard you quite right. You say that whatever this thing was was at my Linda's burial site? Am I hearin' you correctly?"

"That's right," I said. "And not only was the thing, as you say—the UFO or whatever it was—at your wife's gravesite, it was doing something with the grave itself. But that's just a nagging suspicion that Mr. Elliott has. He says he can't prove it cause the fog was so thick that night."

"Where are you right this instant, Mr. Harmless, and what are you doing? Could you possibly meet me in an hour at Pleasant Grove Cemetery?"

I told him I was free and I'd be glad to.

* * *

I arrived at the cemetery early enough to have time to drive slowly through it.

It was one of the bigger graveyards I'd ever visited, with a winding paved road meandering from one section of the premises to another.

A big sign near the entrance laid out the policy on flowers, decorations, and parking.

There must have been thousands of graves—some with large markers with pictures of the deceased and QR codes. Scan the QR code and you'd be taken to a video or website highlighting what the dead person had accomplished in life. Or get pictures of him or her with their family.

Most of the markers, however, were just plain slabs of granite, of varying sizes, with the deceased's name and dates of birth and death.

There were also many graves marked by simple horizontal metal plates—again, with the dead person's name and dates he or she came into this world and then left. Halfway across each plate was an opening suitable for stuffing a flower arrangement, flag, or some other kind of memorial.

And among all the graves—standing like a centerpiece of death—was a large stone mausoleum. A bronze name plate on the outside of one wall announced it as the PLEASANT GROVE CHAPEL MAUSOLEUM.

The mausoleum contained dozens of drawers, many of them with the names of those whose remains were inside.

I kept winding my car slowly through the cemetery and noticed something else among the stained metal plates and granite tombstones. A goodly number of giant pine trees and mature crepe myrtles, many with Spanish moss hanging from them, formed a kind of natural perimeter around the property.

A nice touch for privacy. And those among the dead who loved nature likely would approve.

* * *

I met Randolph Dickinson, husband of the late Linda Sue Dickinson, at our prearranged rendezvous spot—the mausoleum.

The thing that immediately struck me was his height—at least 6 feet 4 inches, I guessed.

The second thing was his demeanor. I'm not an expert on clinical depression but his head drooped downward, in a kind of sad stance, and he had trouble maintaining eye contact. Instead, he tended to stare away from me as if it pained him to connect directly eyeball to eyeball.

We didn't shake hands or even, in this era of COVID, do a fist pump. Instead, he pointed to himself, somewhat weakly, and said his name.

I introduced myself as Lester Harmless, reporter for the Ocean Herald. When I offered to show him my I.D., he waved that off.

"So you were saying that you think someone has disturbed my Linda's gravesite?" he asked.

I quickly summarized what I'd learned from the police report about what the gravedigger said he had witnessed.

"And so this gravedigger said it looked like a UFO, did he?" Dickinson said with a straight face, his eyes making sustained contact with mine for the first time.

I said that seemed to be the case, based on the police report.

"Well, then, let's go have a look at my wife's burial place. Bear in mind, I haven't had time to get a marker on it, but that's been ordered. It'll be here within a month. For now, I just have a small flag there with her name and photo. Linda always liked flags."

We walked maybe 200 yards, through rustling leaves and on a bed of pine needles, to a corner of the cemetery. I was struck by the beauty and peacefulness of the place. And I could understand why he'd chosen to place his wife here.

We got to the spot, a small rectangular shape of freshly planted sod.

But something was amiss because the widower dropped to his knees, as close to the ground as he could get without being on the ground.

While I thought he was clearly depressed when I first met him, he acted more startled now than anything else.

He patted the sod, from one end of the rectangular indentation to the other end, with his two bare hands, squatting and inching himself forward along the way—again from one end of the gravesite to the other end.

"I was here the day after we buried her. It's different here now—somehow. The sod's changed.

He shouted, "And where is the flag and her picture?!"

Chapter 15
Public Conflict

Soon as I got back to the office, I tried calling Miles "Digger" Elliott, the man who had filed the police report about what he said he'd witnessed at Linda Dickinson's gravesite.

No answer and his phone said his voicemail box was filled up.

Curious, I thought, that a grave digger would have had so many calls.

Next, I called the caretaker of Pleasant Grove Cemetery, asking him if the premises had video surveillance.

He said they didn't but were thinking about installing a state-of-the-art system next budget year.

I asked him a few questions about Mr. Elliott.

He said Elliott had been a loyal, hardworking employee for many years, and they'd never had one bit of trouble from him. He always showed up and did what he was paid to do—that being to dig graves and clean up his mess. He had never left any trash or tools at a gravesite. Always left it clean and ready for the burial which the cemetery much appreciated because it had a close working relationship with area funeral homes.

I asked him about the police report filed by Mr. Elliott.

Which elicited a pregnant pause from the cemetery boss.

"Well, I hadn't heard about that, to tell you the truth, so I really can't speak to it," he said uneasily.

"Do you know Mr. Elliott to be a sober, truthful man?"

"Yes, of course," he said.

The conversation grew more tense. So I decided to leave it at that and thanked him for his time.

Next thing I know, I was buzzed by news clerk Rose Jansen—she who never missed a trick and who seemingly had her fingers on everyone's pulse.

"The big man wants to see you ASAP, Lester. I think he and some of the other higher ups at the paper are getting heat over some kind of proposed new development. Something about a New York based company wanting to get some land rezoned close to the ocean."

When I told her that wasn't my beat, Rose reminded me that we were a small newspaper.

"You gotta be flexible and willin' ta do anything here, dear," she said. "Comes with the territory. You read your job description lately? You might want ta take another look at it."

It just so happened that I had a copy in the top drawer of my desk So, irritated, I took it out and reviewed all my designated duties and responsibilities.

They were spelled out clearly:

• Cover courts, police, and crime

• Coverage of agriculture, education, farming, entertainment, and tourism

• Write briefs of upcoming community events and celebrations

•Assist sports department, as needed, in coverage of special competitions or announcements

•Write profile feature stories of compelling personalities in the beach community

And then, at the tail end of my list of duties and responsibilities, there was this catchall bullet point, encompassing God only knows what:

•Other reporting and writing duties as needed or as assigned.

I decided it was likely that way with most job descriptions in small businesses. But I took consolation that one of these days, if I kept my nose clean and did my job well, I'd move to a larger newspaper. And there perhaps I wouldn't be spread so thin.

At least that's what I'd heard from my brethren at larger media properties.

"Just stay there long enough to make a name for yourself in the community and win some awards from the South Carolina Press Association," one close friend had counseled me. "You'll get snatched up pretty quickly by a big paper in Columbia or Charlotte."

Believing that good things come to those who wait patiently and plod along without causing waves, I made my way to the boss's office.

Editor Charles Wallace was on the phone. He didn't look happy.

He motioned for me to have a seat in front of his desk.

Then he finished talking to whoever and slammed the phone down on the receiver.

"You know what, Lester, there's an idiot born every second, and I just got off the line with one. I swear, she was the stupidest woman I've ever heard in my life.

"You ever had to deal with someone like that?"

I didn't know what to say so I just sat there and stared at him.

Which made things worse.

"Well, if you can't answer that question, answer this one, young man. Where are you on all this UFO stuff? Ya turned up any evidence at all?"

"Well, actually, sir, I was about to tell you that…"

"Never mind, Lester," the editor snapped. "We'll deal with that later. For now, I've got something much more pressing. Think of it as a smoldering ember that's threatenin' to catch fire and damage the integrity of this newspaper.

"But that's where you come in, my man. I'm relyin' on you to put folks at ease—or at least as much at ease as is humanly possible in a situation like this."

"And what situation, exactly, is that, sir?" I asked him.

He proceeded to let me know that there was an important public meeting coming up that very evening. A meeting where two groups—one for development and one passionately against it— were scheduled to knock heads.

"It's like this, Lester. I want you to go to that meeting and do your damnedest to make sure that both sides are represented fairly in our newspaper.

"Because, between you and me, a lot of advertising revenue is at stake for our newspaper. If we make one or the other of them angry, it could be devastating to our bottom line."

I countered: "But I thought there was a firewall between editorial and advertising at the Ocean Herald, Sir, meaning we never, ever buckled to the almighty dollar."

Red veins suddenly seemed to pop out of Wallace's thick neck, and his beady eyes got more intense.

"Now don't you try to lecture me on what we do and how we do it, young man! I'll let you know right here and now that there's exceptions to every rule. And this planning and zoning ruckus is one of 'em.

"I'm not askin' you to cave to either side. Just go the extra mile, and then some, to make sure they're both represented in your coverage. Now is that not fair?"

I said it was and asked him a few more questions about the dispute—which he said he didn't know that much about. But the newspaper had a morgue (back issues) that was bound to have information I could use.

"And if you can't find anything there, just ask Rose. She'll know where to look," he said.

And with that, he stood up, took a gulp of coffee from the cup on his desk and opened his office door, waving me out.

"Happy trails, Clark Kent," he cupped his hands whispering to me and smiling as I left. "Maybe you'll run up on a Lois Lane. Who knows?"

* * *

That evening, I found my way to the gymnasium at nearby Socastee Middle School. The Horry County Planning & Zoning Board meeting had been moved to that location because of an expected large crowd.

I arrived a few minutes before the meeting to try to scope the place out and get a feel for what I might encounter.

For sure, it was bound to be something intensely controversial—based on the constant stream of grim-faced people pouring into the gymnasium.

It put me in mind of an old axiom in journalism: when a lot of folks show up for a public meeting, they're not there because they're happy. They're there because they have a fish to fry.

And, indeed, that proved to be the case with this crowd.

I would soon learn that at least 80 percent of the roughly 300 people there lived in an upscale residential community about 3 miles from the ocean. The rest were either residents of a trailer park on the other side of town or they were representatives of a New York based real estate development firm.

The core issue coming before the Zoning & Planning Board: whether to allow the real estate development company to permit trailers, apartments, and condos on 40 acres adjacent to the upscale residential property.

The five male white members of the Z & P Board sat behind a long black table-cloth covered table, a movable microphone in front of each of them. At one end of the table, half furled and on a stand, was an American flag. Immediately in front of the table sat a middle-aged woman, apparently a government employee, typing on a laptop computer.

A lectern with a microphone was situated a few feet away for the benefit of anyone who would address the board.

The audience sat in folding chairs facing the board members.

They were a diverse group in some ways, but 99 percent of them were white, and I guessed most were in at least their 50s.

By diverse, I mean some wore little more than they'd have on at the beach, while others had put on their Sunday best.

First to address the board was an elderly gentleman who kept fiddling with his hearing aids as he walked to the lectern.

He cleared his throat, took a deep breath, as if mustering his courage, and said this:

"My wife and me have lived in Swan Meadows for 20 years and we love it. The reason being, it's a peaceful, beautiful place where we can go for a walk without worrying about our safety. And I've got to tell you that my Ethel and me 're horrified that you'd even consider letting a bunch of apartments and people in trailers move in next to our neighborhood. It would destroy the entire character of Swan Meadows."

Some cheering, interspersed with a few loud jeers, came from the crowd.

Next to speak was a woman who identified herself as president of the Swan Meadows Neighborhood Association. She was sixtyish with short cropped dark hair. She wore a dark blazer with matching skirt. A string of pearls graced her neck. She had eyeglasses attached to her with one of those straps you often see on librarians.

She had obviously come prepared to deliver a long epistle, judging from her stack of notes, some with colored tabs on them.

But the board chairman, sensing that she was about to embark on an overlong presentation, cut her off at the pass.

"Ma'am, we're limiting each speaker to two minutes, so please keep your remarks short and to the point," he said.

"Well, then, I NEVER," she responded, not happy about her time restriction.

She thrust her notes back into a small carrying case. Then she spoke:

"I just want to echo what the previous speaker said about how special a community we have in Swan Meadows. My husband and I couldn't ask for a more tranquil or ideal place to live—such wonderful neighbors and such a clean, pretty neighborhood. All of it would be endangered if you let trailers and apartments and condos and such occupy that acreage next to us."

Next came a lawyerly looking gentleman in his mid-30s. He said he was counsel for the Swan Meadows Neighborhood Association.

"I will let you know," he said, "that we are prepared to go to the South Carolina Supreme Court, if necessary, to block this rezoning request of property next to where I live and where so many of my good friends and neighbors reside. The last thing in the world we need is for a New York real estate development company to come in here and turn our world upside down. You know what will happen if you accede to this company's request, and change the zoning designation of the property in question to allow trailers and apartments?

From a loud booming male voice in the back: Go ahead and tell 'em! "It'll bring in noise. It'll bring in traffic. It'll bring in pollution and trash. And it could potentially bring in...well, you know what kind of people I'm talking about. Therefore, we respectfully petition you tonight to deny this rezoning request now before you."

More cheers from the crowd. But also a barely detectable faint chorus of boos and hisses.

The chairman of the board, intent on not letting things get out of hand, said one more person would be allowed to speak, and if it were someone representing a different perspective, then all the better.

Loud boos from the audience.

A woman with teased hair, tattoos of sea creatures on her arms, and a piercing in her bottom lip made her way to the lectern.

As she approached the front of the room, she glanced back toward the back of the gymnasium where some of her supporters were seated. A few of them waved thumbs-up signs of encouragement.

"First of all," she said, her jaws working fiercely on a piece of gum, "I ain't never done nothin' like this. I'm for sure no public speaker. But I know this. I deeply resent being referred to as trailer trash!"

Silence in the room broken by cheers from the back.

"The fact is none of us live in trailers. They're not called trailers today. They're mobile homes or manufactured housing.

"And maybe y'all wouldn't be so high and mighty to call us—what was it? DEPLORABLES—if you just took a ride over to where we live. We pay our taxes same as you. And we keep our places clean and safe. We don't put up with no foolishness. And we look out for each other."

A lady in the middle of the crowd yelled, "Nobidy said nothin' about y'all bein' deplorables! That was Hillary Clinton talkin' 'bout Trump's voters!"

A well-dressed man in the audience stood up and shouted: "Why are you even here?! You don't even live anywhere near Swan Meadows. You don't care a damn about our neighborhood or our wetlands or our forests!"

A few people sitting in the back, who'd come to the meeting with the woman from the trailer court, rushed to the front to be with her. One of them held up his fists and yelled, "Come on, why don't cha? Who'll be the first to learn the hard way that we're not trailer trash? And we damned sure know how to fight!"

The board members squirmed nervously in their seats, one of them standing up and asking if there was a police officer present.

A uniformed I-mean-business-looking officer walked to the front of the room, put his big hands on his hips, and stood next to the flag.

Meanwhile, the board chairman announced that no action would be taken at that time on the zoning request. Instead, the matter would be taken, he said, "under advisement." Then he said the meeting had been adjourned.

An old man shouted, "What the Sam-hell does under advisement mean?!"

"It means they're just kickin' the can down the road," said the lawyerly man who'd spoken earlier.

With that, I got up and succeeded in interviewing a few of those who'd been seated in the audience.

No one was averse to talking, and each gladly explained to me their positions.

"It ain't that we're against progress," one man emphatically told me. "It's just, why does it have to come at our expense? How would you like to own a $400,000 home and wake up one day and learn a bunch of folks in trailers were movin' near ya?"

Next, to be fair, I sought out one of the people who'd accompanied the group from the trailer court.

I asked him point blank why he had come to the meeting—especially since he didn't live anywhere near Swan Meadows.

His response was, "Because me an' my neighbors had a' sneaky feelin' this was the kind of talk we'd hear—that bein' that some of these uppity New York types would be puttin' us down. They come down here to our beach and buy their big houses and take over our roads and highways. And then they start complainin' about stuff they had up north but don't have here. And before ya know it, you've got one of 'em behind you blowing his damned horn and shakin' his fist like he was drivin' one a' them yellow taxi cabs in the middle of New York City. Me and my friends in our beautiful, well-kept MOBILE HOMES, thank ya, have had just about all we can stand of their high 'n' mighty ways.

We're sick 'n' tired of 'em tryin' ta turn our beach inta the place where they came from.

"So yes, to answer your original question, we sure as hell DID have a great big dog in this damned fight. And we're glad we came tonight."

Satisfied that I had more than enough information to write my story, scheduled to come out in the next morning's edition of the paper, I headed to the exit.

A young lady, who could have been a junior or senior in high school, had apparently been waiting patiently for me.

She introduced herself as Stephanie Wolf, who attended Socastee High School.
"Are you Lester Harmless, the reporter who wrote that article about the UFO? I've been wanting to talk to you," she said.

"Remember the three ladies who said they were taken up into the flying saucer?"

When I said I did recall them but couldn't rattle off their names at that instant, she said she understood.

She added, "I just want you to know that my family has known them for a very long time, and they are definitely not liars. They are good, upstanding, church-going women who don't have anything to gain by cookin' up some wild story about bein' taken up into a flyin' saucer."

I thanked her and asked if I could have the names and cell numbers of her parents, which she gave me.

"Keep writing and don't let anybody shoo you off that story. PLEASE, Mr. Harmless. You've got more people than you can imagine on your side."

Chapter 16
A Grave Matter

Early the next morning, I woke up to a scratchy voicemail from Miles "Digger" Elliott.

He said he'd been out of town on a hunting trip. But now he'd be glad to meet with me.

At the cemetery at 10 that morning, I pulled up alongside his white dented up old van.

One of the side windows in his vehicle was cracked and duct tape kept the left front headlight from falling apart.

Stained Styrofoam™ coffee cups, broken plastic spoons, crushed water bottles, candy wrappers, and crumpled packs of Camel cigarettes, along with a fair number of butts, lined the cracked dashboard.

Splotches of white drab paint had peeled off the van, leaving plenty of places where you saw only the bare metal.

On top of it was a rack which held a ladder, picks, and shovels.

Despite all that, both sides of the vehicle were emblazoned with a fairly catchy logo in giant red and blue letters: "GRAVES MATTER—If you don't believe it, wait'll you die!"

Getting out of his van, Digger extended his open right hand—not his fist.

"You must be the newspaperman, Lester Harmless. Glad ta meet ya."

Then he looked at his van, leaned up against it, and said proudly, "I know it's a BEATER but it does me just fine, thank ya. Wouldn't have anything else even if I could."

He was the first professional grave digger I'd ever met, and if there were a formula for the kind who did his line of work, he matched it to a tee.

He was short, but muscular with broad shoulders, thick forearms, a humped back, and calloused large hands. He had long fingernails with dirt caked under them, a shock of unkept gray hair, and a ruddy bearded face. Unsightly hairs dangled from his nose.

In his mouth, behind two yellow front teeth, he chewed on a wad of snuff, spitting out a disgusting slurp every now and then to the side.

He wore dirty bib overalls and an old blue denim shirt with sweat stains under his armpits. On his feet were a pair of muddy work boots.

Although I tried hard not to stare at him, I must have failed because he laughed, nudged his discolored ball cap slightly backward, and said, "Now what can I do fer ya taday, young man? By the way, welcome ta my office."

I returned his smile and started the conversation by asking him how long he'd been a grave digger.

He seemed eager to talk about himself.

"Well, to start off with, a lotta folks think that what I do is kinda creepy or spooky. But ya know what? I downright like it!

"For one thing, I like bein' outdoors in the fresh air and sunshine, and even when the sun ain't shinin', I still like what I do. I tried factory work an' hated it. Too many people and too much pressure. Out here, I'm among my friends. I call 'em my sleepin' brothers and sisters. It's just me an' them and the squirrels and a few rabbits. Nobidy ta talk to or have ta put up with, and that's just the way I like it.

"And I want ta say somethin' else. My line a' work really matters to folks, and if it don't matter now, it will one day down the road. Cause, Mister, we all die. As the Good Book says, 'From Dust ta Dust.'"

I asked him how many graves he dug every day and he said that on a good day, working alone, he could get two graves done—each of them six feet deep and a little over three feet wide.

"Course, how many I get dug in a single day just depends," he added. "On things like how many tree roots or rocks I run into. Or how hard or wet the ground is.

"On our coldest days, it can be mighty tough diggin'. Ya ever tried ta stick a shovel inta the icy ground?"

While I said I had never done that, I told him I could well imagine how hard it could be.

I steered the conversation toward the police report.

"So you say, Mr. Elliott, that you were out here a few nights ago, all night long. Why would you be spending the night in your van here at the cemetery?"

"It ain't somethin' I normally do," he assured me, "but that perticular evenin', I was too tard to drive home, and I always keep a piller and blankets and extra food, drinks, and such in my van, just in case, and so, I just decided to kinda camp out over there under that giant live oak tree."

He pointed to an ancient, towering oak tree with Spanish moss majestically hanging from its thick limbs. The tree stood at the eastern edge of the graveyard, seemingly holding vigil against the nearby marshland and swamp and providing shade for dozens of gravesites.

From that spot, I concluded he'd have a clear, unobstructed view of Linda Sue Dickinson's burial place.

"So tell me about that night, Mr. Elliott. You said on the police report that you saw something very unusual."

"Indeed I did. Indeed I did, Mr. Harmless. In fact, ain't never seen nothin' like it in my life. To start with, 'twas a beautiful night. Full moon and sky full of twinklin' stars."

I interrupted him.

"Back up a minute, please, Sir. If you were asleep, what woke you up? How was it that you were even conscious when you saw what you say you saw?"

"Because fer one thing, you ever tried sleepin' in a beat-up old van? Ain't the most comfortable place ta rest, I'll tell ya that. You don't believe me; you try sleepin' in it!

"So I woke up fer a spell ta go pee, and I'd just finished my business and zipped up when, damn, I saw a sight ta behold!

"It was big, I mean REAL BIG, an' round and bright orange. Like a big ol' ball hangin' in the air, and it wuz d'rectly hoverin' over that grave I'd just dug before callin' it a day and packin' up my tools.

"And it was quiet as a mouse. Not even a buzz or hum or nothin'. That's what really skeered me. Somethin' that big and bright hangin' in the air quiet as a ghost, it seemed."

"And so you're saying you yourself had dug Linda Sue Dickinson's grave that day?"

"Yep, cause I'd done met her husband a couple days previously. A sad, sad man he was, too.

"He gave me special instructions on how he wanted his wife's grave dug. Not like I get such from most folk. They leave me be ta do my work fer the funeral home."

"Instructions, you say?"

"Yep. For one thing, he wanted it dug about two feet deeper than normal. Said he'd pay for my extra work."

"Any other special requests from him?"

"Yep. Said he wanted the head of her casket to be outta the bright sunlight. Said his wife never took kindly to bein' out'n the sun. Even at the beach, she stayed under the umbrella. Hated getting tanned or burned."

"So how'd you accommodate that?"

"I made danged sure the funeral home knew which way to place her casket. They promised me they'd do it that way."

"Okay. So back to what you saw. That big bright orange ball, as you say. Did it do anything other than just hover over the gravesite?"

"Yes and no. And I say that cause I don't know for certain what it did or didn't do. Ya see, it had a thick mist or fog or something like that coming out of its downside. Sa thick ya couldn't see the ground d'rectly beneath it. Like a beam of some kind or another—best way I'd describe it."

"And so how long did it just stay there?"

He estimated no longer than 10 minutes at the most, and maybe even less than that.

"Then, whoosh! It was gone lickity split. Like I blinked my eye and it wasn't there no more. And, again, no sound at all. No motor. No rumble. Nothing at all like a jet or airplane. More like it just dissolved inta the night."

I probed him about that pint of bourbon he mentioned on the police report.

Yes, he'd been sipping on it, but no, he said, he was not intoxicated. Just said he partook of it as a nightcap—to help him relax.

"And so you're sayin' to me that you were an eyewitness to a flying saucer? Do I have that correct?"

"I ain't sayin' nothin' of the sort! I ain't havin' no idear what the heck that was that I saw. Except I know this. I don't lie and I don't cheat and I don't dream crap up. And I don't mind at all if you ask around about me. I'm an honest, simple man who digs in the ground practic'ly ever day of my life. Ain't tryin' to impress nobidy or get nobidy's attention. Just doin' my job—day in and day out."

I thanked him again for agreeing to meet with me and asked if he'd walk with me to Linda Sue Dickinson's grave.

Which he gladly did, but also, for whatever reason, a bit warily.

"I ain't been back there since the day I dug it," he said. "And it ain't that I'm afeerd to go back. It's just, well, never mind. Let's go check it out."

We made our way slowly through the rustling leaves, stepping carefully over protruding roots from the giant live oak tree which shaded this part of the cemetery. About 50 Canadian geese, flying in formation, honked loudly in the partly cloudy sky above us. And I thought, as we walked, that I could smell the salt air from the ocean, which, from this location, was at least 20 miles away. And if it wasn't the salt air, it was some kind of scent coming from the swamp not far from us.

Curious, I thought, that so many souls were resting so close to alligators and cottonmouth water moccasins.

Still, however, Pleasant Grove Cemetery was truly a beautiful place. It seemed to have it all: peacefulness, tranquility, undisturbed nature (for the most part), and a genuine sense that you could come here and meditate or be close to your loved one (now lying in the ground or in a mausoleum crypt).

The kind of place, I thought, that I'd like to be buried or have my cremains stored for posterity.

Not that I ordinarily dwelled that much on death, but recently I'd worked on a few obituary notices at the paper. So if death wasn't exactly top of my mind, it was as if there was a little voice inside my brain whispering to me to get my affairs in order.

In due time, I kept telling myself. *In due time.*

Meanwhile, we had arrived at the gravesite in question.

Mr. Elliott, like Linda Sue Dickinson's husband, dropped to his knees. Then he took off his ball cap and ran the backside of a rough right hand over his forehead.

"Well, I'll beeeeeeee..." he said, drawing out his last word.

"Somethin's been done ta the ground here. It ain't like I left it. That's for sure."

He dug down a few inches with a pocketknife, then stopped.

"Somebidy or some thing's been tamperin' with this grave. I know it cause when I dig a hole and fill 'er up, I have my own way a' doin' it. It's kinda like my signature. And lookee here at this sod. I never laid this sod like that. It's laid sideways and slanted. Mine's always up and down. How da ya call it?"

"Vertical?" I asked.

"Zactly!" he said.

"Since I packed this sod in, somebidy's peeled it off and put it back sideways. Now why would they do such a thing?

"Unless."

"Unless what?" I asked.

"Lest they dug her back up!"

Chapter 17
Trouble Sleeping

I left the graveyard just in time to grab a bite to eat before hightailing it down to Surfside Beach.

A polar bear plunge in the Atlantic Ocean was to occur at 2 p.m. across the street from a popular bar and grill.

I arrived at the bar and grill shortly after 1 o'clock and found it full of folks, many of them already stripped down to their swimsuits or to shorts and tee-shirt. They were toasting each other and guzzling beer, wine, margaritas, and shots of bourbon—all of it to prepare for the icy dip in the ocean.

Well, not icy exactly, because it was Myrtle Beach. Even in early January, the beach doesn't come near to getting as cold as, say, a lake in Minnesota or Canada.

Today, the air temperature at our beach was 57 degrees, with the water being also in the high fifties.

Way too cold for me to swim in the ocean, but not so unbearable as to deter about 75 hearty souls from taking a dip in the sea to help fund a new non-profit no-kill animal shelter in our area.

Each of them had paid a registration fee of $10—with many forking out way more than that to help fund the planned new animal shelter—to swim in the ocean.

As I made my way, with my notebook and recorder, among the happy and soon-to-be-soaked-from-the-ocean revelers at the bar and grill, I asked them the same questions.

Why are you doing this?

Are you really going to jump into the ocean in a few minutes, and, if so, will you go completely under the water?

How do you get ready for something like this?

Some of their responses surprised me.

"What's the big deal? I go swimming every day in the ocean. I was down here swimming yesterday. The water temperature here feels like New Jersey in the summer." (from a 78-year-old man)

"You gotta do what you gotta do and then get outta the ocean. Anything ta help them poor little dogs and cats." (from a 49-year-old woman who said she worked as a property manager for a real estate company)

"I tell all my friends who're doing this that when they run into the ocean, be sure to keep their mouths closed. Cause if you run in screamin' and laughin', water'll gush into your mouth. And you definitely ain't wantin' that!" (Business owner, age 36).

One woman shared with me that the best way to train for something like this is to drink a lot of tequila.

All of it, along with a few pictures I snapped with my iPhone, good human interest material for the article I wrote later that day.

Back at my office, I finished my polar bear plunge story fairly quickly and decided to touch base with my editor, Charles Wallace.

As usual, he was chatting on the phone, with his thick legs propped up and crossed on one end of his huge desk.

He motioned me to take a seat, cupping the phone and turning his head briefly to whisper to me that he wouldn't be long.

"So what's up, Lester?" he asked me snidely after he was done with the phone call. "Somebody said you went swimming in the ocean. If so, I hope you had somebody waitin' for you with a big blanket. Pretty damned cold out there for a white man to be takin' a dip today.

"I never said that, by the way," he added.

I laughed just the same and let him know that I'd never go in the ocean in the dead of winter— regardless of what the good cause might be.

"I guess I know that, Lester. You're a smart man. I'm just pullin' your string."

Exactly what that meant, I wasn't sure, but I just shrugged and started to make my way for the door.

"Sit back down, if you don't mind, please," my boss said, pointing toward my chair. "While you're here, I want you to tell me the latest about the flyin' saucers. And don't hold anything back. Because I have to confess, you got a lot of folks riled up with your story about Ted Staley not requesting that

179

those Air Force fighter jets be scrambled. We sold every damned print paper we put out that edition, and the traffic on our website went through the roof. And of, course, the schnooks working in advertising loved it. Because, the more eyeballs we get on a story, the better and easier it is for them to do their job.

"It's all about the eyeballs, Lester. So if you've got anything else about those flyin' saucers in the old hopper, don't hold back on me.

"So tell me," said editor Wallace, his expression growing more serious, his jaw tightening and his eyes squinting, "you got anything else?"

"I may have something soon, Sir, but I'm not ready to write it—just yet."

"So what does 'just yet' mean, exactly?" he shot back. "Whatever it is, we sure as hell don't want to get scooped on it, do we? You understand my drift? Because there's an old saying: He who hesitates is lost!"

I promised him that within the week, I should have enough material to bring to him for pre-approval. For now, though, I asked him to bear with me just a bit longer.

"I promise you, Sir, that this'll make a far bigger splash than my other story."

"That good, is it? Well now, you've got my curiosity up. Go in peace, my man, and get your ducks in order and bring them back to me. From what you're saying, this'll be damned juicy and interesting. Exactly the kind of shot in the arm that the Ocean Herald needs!"

I left his office with a flurry of jumbled thoughts. One, I'd promised something that I HOPED I could deliver. Two, he was practically salivating for another UFO story—this from a hardened, skeptical man who'd told me again and again that he thought UFOs were a grand hoax. Three, and most importantly, what the heck was I supposed to write, exactly? Something about a local gravesite allegedly being disturbed by aliens from outer space?!

* * *

After completing some routine assignments and double-checking with Rose, our news clerk, that no late breaking news had occurred warranting my attention, I made my way home.

I lived in a small bungalow within a stone's throw, almost, of the beach. It wasn't fancy but I loved it for the privacy—no neighbors within a couple hundred yards—and nothing but a long dune between me and the wide scenic beach.

I quickly changed into more casual clothes and walked down to the beach. Always a good place to clear my mind and escape, if only temporarily, the pressures of work.

Today, as I wandered slowly on the tightly packed sand near the ocean because that made for easier walking, I noticed two guys surf fishing. One was standing in the waves, while the other was at water's edge. Both had big saltwater rods and reels and they wore rubberized bib overalls and up-to-their hips wading boots. Next to them was a beach wagon stocked, I was certain, with bait and refreshments.

I asked them if they'd had any luck.

"Nothin' so far, but who really cares?" the shorter one replied with a grin.

"It's all about just being out here in the sunshine with the waves, isn't it?" I said.

They both nodded and one of them managed a "I guess so, if that's how you wanna put it. But sure would be nice to land a big fish. Ain't matterin' what kind it is. Just somethin' fit ta eat."

I kept on walking, taking in the full magic of the ocean, waves, salt air, sand, shells, and wind.

It never seemed to grow old—this place that had been named Myrtle Beach early in the last century and that had been a favorite getaway for so many people for so long.

Today, just beyond where the waves broke onto the shore, a dolphin teasingly bobbed up and down. I kept my eyes on this beautiful animal for about 20 minutes wondering where he was headed.

It didn't really matter where, I decided. What mattered was that he'd decided to give me a glimpse of his majesty. And what a beautiful sea creature! So smart. Even maybe smarter, I'd read, than any other animal in the ocean. And able to communicate with other dolphins miles away. An animal that had been known to save drowning sailors at sea.

And there he (or maybe she) was, giving me a show. Something restful and magnificent for me to dwell on as I nodded off to slumberland later tonight.

Before then, however, I had to have a plan.

The boss expected me to produce another story about UFOs, of all things, and I'd promised him it was coming.

One idea: pursue the disturbed gravesite angle.

Yes, in one way it was farfetched. Especially given that the supposed eyewitness had been drinking when, as he put it, a huge round object had hovered above and then descended within a few feet of Linda Sue Dickinson's final resting place.

But the gravedigger had seemed entirely credible when I'd spoken to him earlier today.

And what to make of the deceased's grieving husband, Randolph Dickinson?

Both he and the gravedigger were absolutely sure that the burial plot had been altered.

I had grilled them repeatedly on that.

And they stood by their stance that the gravesite had been changed. No question about it, they had said.

Which was intriguing, to be sure, but not enough to warrant a full-fledged story in the newspaper.

Unless it could be established that the change somehow came from a UFO—the strange orange ball of light that Elliott had said he'd seen.

But how to come up with such proof?

* * *

Late that night, I lay awake restless and uneasy. But instead of counting sheep to get to sleep, I decided on dolphins.

Something about dwelling on that wonderful creature bobbing up and down just beyond the waves helped me nod off.

But sleep wasn't pleasant.

Instead of my subconscious being on dolphins, I had shifted to a vision of the moist, damp dirt and freshly laid sod that marked Linda Sue Dickinson's grave.

185

And among those layers of sod, coming out of the porous recently dug ground, were cankerworms and maggots.

The bony fingers of a pale, rotting, shrouded corpse had clawed their way out of the grave and seemed to be crying out in desperation.

The voice was that of a terrified woman.

"Save me! I'm smothering down here! There's nothing but rottenness and blackness and the stench of death! Get me out of this tomb!"

I woke up with a jolt in a cold sweat and sat on the edge of my bed. It was 4 a.m. and I wouldn't be getting any more sleep.

All that stuff about a putrid corpse trying to claw its way out of a grave!

Nothing but a nightmare of the first order.

Yep, that's all it had been.

Or had it been trying to point me toward some one or some thing?

I decided that tomorrow I'd pay another visit to Linda Sue Dickinson's husband.

Chapter 18
Fuss Over A Corpse

The next day I rendezvoused with the widower, Randolph Dickinson, at a picnic shelter at Huntington Beach State Park. He said he often hung out there to commune with the seagulls, egrets, bald eagles, and alligators.

If you were lucky and were able to drive slowly enough across the bridge into the park, without an impatient motorist behind you leaning on his horn, you'd see an alligator.

Today, I spotted two big gators—their snouts barely above the surface of the marshy water. Occasionally, you'd see them swim out to an island and sun themselves to sleep. Or at least they appeared to be sleeping. You never knew for sure with a gator. It was always best to view the unpredictable bulging-eyed reptiles from a safe distance.

As I approached Dickinson, I noticed he had a stack of papers on the picnic table next to where he sat. As I got closer, they appeared to be legal documents. He had them laid out neatly in piles, so that apparently he'd be able to pull whatever sheet of paper he needed while we spoke.

We shook hands, exchanged pleasantries and got down to business.

I let him know that I'd made another trip to the cemetery—this time to speak with the man who'd dug his wife's grave.

"And did he tell you it had been tampered with?" he asked.

I told him that for sure, Mr. Elliott said his wife's grave had been changed.

"Just as I suspected!" Dickinson responded. His face reddened and his eyes narrowed. "That THING in the sky—or whatever it was that the grave digger saw—messed with my wife's body. It somehow penetrated the ground and did something to the corpse.

"And I intend to find out what," he emphasized, pointing to the stack of papers.

He explained that they had been drawn up, at considerable expense, by a lawyer in Myrtle Beach. They would be presented to a judge requesting that a court order be executed for exhumation of Linda Sue Dickinson's corpse.

189

He asked me how likely it'd be that the judge would agree to such a request?

Before I could respond, Dickinson said that exhumations were rare in South Carolina, as they were throughout America.

"And even if a judge agrees to order one," he said, "opening a grave is enormously expensive and is often done as a last resort in a criminal case or to resolve some kind of potentially intractable dispute.

"In my case, I'm arguing that there's a good chance my wife's remains have been desecrated. Or that her corpse has maybe even been stolen," Dickinson said, his mouth seeming to tighten.

"But by whom or what?" I asked.

"Possibly by aliens or whatever it was in that spacecraft that Mr. Elliott witnessed. All I know is that some being or creature, quite possibly an alien from another world, penetrated my wife's grave the other night. And I want to know what they did to her body."

The distraught man went on to tell me that there's a hefty fine and stiff prison sentence for anyone found guilty of harming, stealing, or desecrating a corpse in South Carolina.

"And for all I know, my beloved wife's not even still in her grave. They mighta' took her!" he shouted. "But why, of all people, my Linda? Whad' she ever do to deserve this?"

"So, no pun intended, but is this pretty much an open and shut case?" I asked. "You confident a judge will issue that exhumation order?"

Dickinson told me that it wasn't a given and that his wife's younger sister, Robin Jones, had voiced her strong opposition to an exhumation.

The anxious man frowned and said bitterly: "She's been a pain in the royal ass all her life, and so it was to be expected that she'd be against me on this. She's never liked me since Day 1. But my Linda always took her side. Guess that old sayin's right. 'Blood's thicker'n water. Go figure."

We parted ways but not before he allowed me to quickly read the documents he'd brought with him. He also permitted me to photograph a few of the more important ones.

And I learned that Linda's sister, Robin, intended to fight tooth and nail to keep her sister's gravesite undisturbed.

"The thing is, she'll do everything in her power to stop me," Dickinson groused. "And not only her, but she's bound to win over a bunch of her friends at Salt and Light Church of the Third Nazarene."

"You attend there with your wife?"

"Hardly ever, except for C and E?"

"C and E?"

"Christmas and Easter," he said, keeping a straight face. "And that was about it. But not my Linda. She loved that church more than just about anything in the world. Sunday School classes, small groups, youth program, Ladies Prayer Shawl Ministry, retreats for the women, Sunday and Wednesday worship services. You name it. If the church doors were open, Linda'd be there."

"But you yourself pretty much avoided that place. Is that correct?"

"Let's just say I've never been a very social person. Least not like Linda. She loved people. Me, on the other hand, I've been content to stay in my own bubble, away from crowds. And, I hate sayin' this, but every church has its fair share of backbiters and hypocrites. I'd rather just go it alone. I've always, in that respect, been a lone wolf."

"So where might I find Robin Jones?"

"You really want to know? Go to that church. I guarantee you she'll be there."

* * *

So, it being Wednesday evening, I decided to pay a visit to the Salt and Light Church of the Third Nazarene in Murrells Inlet, a short drive from the ocean. A sign at the church entrance announced: LIFE IS HARD BUT GOD IS GOOD.

It struck me as a fairly modern structure and I quickly learned that it offered two services on Sunday morning—one a contemporary gathering featuring modern Christian music and the other traditional with the old time-tested hymns.

Because it was Wednesday, churchgoers had access to a chicken dinner meal with all the trimmings, compliments of the youth ministry, before taking their seats in folding chairs facing a stage at the front of the spacious auditorium.

I was greeted by at least four people—all of them shaking my hand or patting me on the back and welcoming me warmly.

"And please go to the front of the line and get yourself a plate," one young woman said. "It's free and we want you to make yourself at home."

"This is what we do every Wednesday before the preacher takes to the pulpit," an older gentleman smiled and said. "Because, after all, we're Nazarenes at heart. So we eat 'n meet ever' chance we get, the good Lord willin'."

After I'd eaten—or "filled my hide," as my beloved mom would have put it, I found a seat near the stage. I decided that I'd take in the sermon before I tried to cop a quick interview with Robin Jones. I'd met her briefly at the table where I'd eaten but had not yet told her that I was from the newspaper. That could wait.

The church service started predictably enough. There was no choir but a bearded, shaggy, jeans-clad song leader with a silver ponytail and speckled long-sleeved untucked shirt got the worshippers on their feet and clapping. He started with a spirited rendition of "The Old Rugged Cross" which was followed by a hit Christian rock song "I Can Only Imagine." Behind him on the stage were two other guitar players, a drummer, and a keyboard player.

Following that was an opening long prayer by the lean, trim, short-haired pastor, who, as far as I could discern, was well thought of by his congregants. They seemed to hang on his every word and kept their eyes shut and heads bowed until he said "Amen."

I was startled when he yielded the microphone and lectern over to none other than Robin Jones.

She was an attractive woman in her mid-50s with shoulder-length auburn hair, green eyes, and perfect white teeth. She was in a grey pant suit and blue blouse that hugged her figure. And somehow her shoes, which struck me as the type you'd work out in at a fitness center, seemed to be just the right choice for the occasion.

After her first few words, which immediately caught my attention, I pulled out my notebook and turned my iPhone recorder on, hoping that it'd pick up what she said.

"Ladies and gentlemen of Salt and Light Church, I'm sure you all remember my dear beloved sister—Linda Sue Dickinson. And I haven't had a chance to thank each of you personally for everything you did for her husband, my brother-in-law, Randolph, when she recently died. All the phone calls, all your cards and letters, and your food...God is good!

"So let me start by giving you all THANKS right now, right here and saying y'all went far above and beyond in all your kindness for me and my brother-in-law. I told him about our service tonight but, as you know, he's the shy, bashful type. But he thanks you from the bottom of his bashful little broken heart.

"Which brings me to a sensitive point. Y'all know my sister Linda is interred at Pleasant Grove Cemetery not too far from here, and in fact, many of you attended her service there.

"And you know, if you happened to be there, that after praying on my sister's coffin, and reading a few final words of farewell from Ecclesiastes in the Bible, they lowered her into the ground.

"Six feet down into the ground, in fact," Robin noted.

"More like 7 or 8 feet, it seemed to me," I heard an old timer sitting behind me whisper to his wife.

"Hush," she reprimanded him.

"Well, I must say it was a beautiful service—for what it was," Robin continued. "We were fortunate that day to have sunny weather and a blue sky and I couldn't help but notice the squirrels scampering back and forth in a nearby live oak tree. And then those brilliant daffodils that seemed to have just sprung up out of the good Lord's earth. Everything was wonderful, for what it was.

"And there was a little boy there—and forgive me cause I didn't get his name. But he dropped a beautiful red rose down into the ground where they'd lowered by sister. And he blew her a kiss. It touched my heart, ladies and gentlemen.

"But now, and this is the painful part of what I must share with you, my brother-in-law, Randolph Dickinson, has got it in his mind that he wants my sister Linda's body exhumed from her grave!"

Stunned gasps, astounded looks, and jostling came from the congregation.

"Yes, you heard me right, brothers and sisters. Randolph is going to court to ask a judge for permission to let him dig up my sister's corpse."

"Why on earth's he doin' that," came a loud, piercing question from the rear of the sanctuary.

A woman blurted out, "Has he lost his mind?!"

Robin let the crowd's murmurings simmer down while she gulped a long swig from a water bottle.

Then she grimaced, faced her listeners, and without missing a beat said this: "Because my brother-in-law thinks some little green men in a flyin' saucer did something awful to my sister's body!"

"Well, ain't that the damnedest thing," a man yelled while his wife tried frantically to muzzle him.

"Sylvester! Watch your language. You're in the Lord's House," she said, nudging him sharply with her left elbow.

Robin Jones seemed not to have heard any of this, or, if she did, she paid it no mind.

She ended by saying she promised to let everyone know the date and time the court would rule on the exhumation request.

"And if you could be there to show support for me and my sister so that she'll continue to rest in peace and her remains not be disturbed..."

She couldn't finish the sentence before the congregation roared its pledge to be at the court proceeding.

A man sitting in the front row grabbed the microphone and said, "Judges in this county get elected by the people, so we can make a difference! And Linda Sue Dickinson was one of our own. If they can dig 'er up, they can do the same for me'r you or our kin."

With that, Robin Jones handed the microphone to the church's pastor. He read a few short verses from Scripture pertaining to how to mourn for the dead and gave the benediction.

The congregation then burst out, spontaneously it seemed to me, in a thunderous singing of "Amazing Grace."

That was followed by the hymn "I'll Fly Away" accompanied by foot stomping and hand clapping.

Curious, I wondered why they'd be singing a song about flying away, given the controversy about UFOs.

Everyone filed out of the church but not before saying their farewells—some with hugs—to Robin Jones who stationed herself at the church exit along with the pastor. She occasionally dabbed her eyes with a tissue.

As I left and shook her hand, I still hadn't had a chance to properly identify myself to Robin. It didn't seem to be the right time or place—what with so many congregants behind me waiting in line to bid her good-bye and good luck. Hugs, tears and kisses were plentiful.

Chapter 19
Breaking The News

Back the next morning in the newsroom of the Ocean Herald, I emailed my editor requesting a top priority conference.

Which got a rapid response from him asking for the reason.

I described, as best I could in a few sentences, what I'd learned from my two interviews at the cemetery. And I gave him a quick summary of what had occurred at last night's church service.

He must have been at his computer and eagerly reading every word because he said he was requesting a meeting of four people—myself, himself, the executive editor of the newspaper, and the CEO of the paper—the publisher.

One hour later, the four of us sat in editor Charles Wallace's office. All eyes were on me after the publisher and executive editor (the latter clad in Bermuda shorts and in a loose polo shirt, as if he'd just come from a golf course) motioned for me to fill them in.

Which I did, giving them a somewhat more nuanced account of what I'd already told Wallace via email.

I let the three of them know I could write another UFO-story based on the information I'd gleaned from the grave digger and the widower of the late Linda Sue Dickinson.

But I had uneasy feelings about writing what I'd heard and observed at the church service.

"But you took good notes, didn't you?"

"Of the church service, yes," I replied. "And I'm sure I captured much of it with the audio recorder app on my iPhone."

"So what's the problem?" publisher Barbara Huntington wondered. She took off her glasses, fetched a lens cleaner from her purse, and proceeded to clean them carefully.

Her son, the executive editor, meanwhile had perked up slightly when he heard the word "UFO," and now looked alert to what I might say next.

"So you attended this church and you're saying you didn't get a chance to identify yourself as a member of the press. Have I got that about right, Lester," Wallace asked gruffly.

"And now you're worried about performing your professional duty as a reporter just because why? Explain that to us again, please."

"Because it's almost like I was a spy on their private church service. To me, if I write what I learned there, it won't pass the smell test."

Wallace stared at me and pursed his lips with exasperation.

"And so how much of this so-called uneasiness on your part has to do with the fact that they provided you dinner and gave you a royal churchy warm welcome," the editor asked snidely.

He hit a nerve.

"It's just that I was in their church. They trusted me and welcomed me with open arms. And what am I supposed to do—embarrass them in the newspaper? People might've said things they wouldn't 'uv said had they known a reporter sat among them."

The publisher asked why on earth would I think I'd be embarrassing them.

"After all, about how many people would you say attended that service last night?" she asked.

"A little over a hundred," I estimated.

"And so how many of them, my dear, would you say have Facebook accounts or Twitter or Instagram?"

I began to sense where this was going and just shrugged my shoulders and looked away from her.

"Nobody in this room knows, Lester," Wallace sternly interjected. "Furthermore, it's impossible for us to know whether anyone else in that crowd also took notes or recorded the service.

"But odds are someone did. And I'll lay better than even odds that someone has already blown the whistle or blabbed about the church service on social media.

"Which makes your supposed uneasiness all the more ridiculous, wouldn't you say?"

In response, the only thing I could think of had to do with two wrongs not making something right.

"And for some reason, a blogger or Facebooker's not the same as a professional reporter infiltrating a private worship service," I noted.

Which aroused the normally taciturn publisher.

"Why do you say 'infiltrate' and why do you keep using that phrase 'private church service,' she asked, "when you yourself have said at least a hundred folks were there?"

I struggled to answer her.

But Wallace explained it better than I ever could.

"He doesn't mean to really call it 'private' because anyone on earth could have walked into that church and taken in their service. So in that respect, the service occurred in a very public place, not behind locked doors or at a private residence. And he didn't 'infiltrate' anything. That church welcomes anyone.

"So anything said there last night is fair game for whoever wants to write about it. We would definitely NOT be invading anyone's privacy by publishing a story of the proceedings. It'd be like me sitting on a public beach or in a park and taking note of all I saw and heard and then writing about it. The First Amendment gives me that right. Now does anyone disagree with me?"

The publisher beginning to smile, smoothed her skirt, rose from her chair, and nodded no.

The executive editor had minutes ago been focused on his cell phone, as if he were checking on a tee time. He mumbled something unintelligible about UFOs and wished me well.

Editor Wallace smacked his hands together, grinned, and acted like he'd prevailed in a battle of strong-willed professionals.

"Guess this means we've got a dandy of another flyin' saucer story comin' from you, Lester. So get going on it. I'll tease this one in a skybox (an attention-getting logo above the newspaper's nameplate) on the front page. And I'll order an increased press run. Because we definitely don't want to sell out of newspapers!

"And if you've got any ideas for an illustration or a picture of some kind to help pull readers into your piece, shoot those to me. I'll get our graphic artist working on it soon as possible."

I hurried back to my desk, quickly scanned my notes and began writing. I decided that this was a piece that would almost write itself. After all, I had the information from my interviews with Randolph Dickinson and the grave digger (Miles "Digger" Elliott). And I had an abundance of stuff from the church service.

The crucial question was how to open the story. With the UFO? Or should that part be downplayed or even omitted altogether?

Not a hard decision.

I quickly decided on what my boss and even his boss (the publisher) wanted me to emphasize.

By Lester Harmless
General Assignment Reporter
The Ocean Herald

A strange, glowing, ball-shaped object hovered over a recently dug grave at Pleasant Grove Cemetery a few miles south of Conway for several minutes shortly after midnight earlier this week.

The self-described astounded man who witnessed the huge orange airborne ball, which he described as an Unidentified Flying Object (UFO), was veteran grave digger Miles "Digger" Elliott.

Elliott had dug the grave, the final resting place for car crash victim Linda Sue Dickinson of Myrtle Beach, just a few hours earlier.

Mrs. Dickinson's graveside funeral service had been held, her husband and other mourners had said their farewells, and the casket had been lowered into the ground.

That evening, after Elliott had closed the grave up, the grave digger said he was exhausted. So he decided to spend the night in his van just a few yards from Mrs. Dickinson's gravesite.

A few minutes after midnight, he woke up and saw what he described in a police report as a "big orange flyin' somethin' like one a' them UFOs you hear 'bout in tha news."

He said the ball-shaped object was huge, appeared to be other worldly, and lingered about 10-15 feet above the recently closed up gravesite for about 10 minutes.

He added that the object projected a beam of light onto the grave but it was difficult to see if the beam penetrated the ground because of the dense night fog.

Then the object left the scene silently—with only a "whoosh"—and at hypersonic speed.

Upon looking closely at the gravesite a few days later, Elliott is convinced that something was done to alter Mrs. Dickinson's final resting place.

The deceased's husband, Randolph Dickinson, is of the same opinion. He suspects that the UFO's beam of light somehow penetrated his wife's grave and may have done something to her corpse—perhaps even removing it.

So the grief-stricken Mr. Dickinson has hired a lawyer and filed a motion in Horry County District Court for a judge to issue an order of exhumation of his wife's body.

That is the only way, he says, that he'll know for sure whether anything inappropriate has been done to her corpse. Or even if her body is still where it was buried in Pleasant Grove Cemetery.

Meanwhile, the congregation at the late Mrs. Dickinson's home church, Salt and

Light Church of the Third Nazarene at
Murrells Inlet, is strongly opposed to
having her body exhumed.

Churchgoers there dismiss as absurd the
notion that a UFO from outer space
somehow tampered with Mrs. Dickinson's
gravesite.

And they are adamant in their belief
that her corpse should not be dug up
but that instead it should be allowed
to rest in peace at the cemetery.

A coalition of Mrs. Dickinson's close
friends and fellow churchgoers have
pledged to show up at the court
exhumation hearing and to make their
voices loudly heard.

Leading the exhumation/opposition group
is Robin Jones, sister of the deceased
Mrs. Dickinson. Jones publicly stated
at a recent church evening service that
her brother-in-law, Randolph Dickinson,
believes "some little green men in a
flyin' saucer did something awful to
her sister's body!"

That assertion was met with a chorus of
loud boos and jeers from the
congregation. And one man in attendance
stood up and yelled, "Linda Sue
Dickinson was one of our own. If they
can dig 'er up, they can do the same
for me'r you or our kin!"

210

Which was followed at the church service by a hearty outburst of "Amens!"

Incredible as it seems to some skeptics, the sighting of a UFO at Pleasant Grove Cemetery follows another UFO sighting a few weeks ago at Surfside Beach. Two people surf fishing there, along with dozens of others on the beach, said they saw a mysterious orange ball of light, as big as a house, in the sky above the ocean. It, too, made absolutely no sound and appeared to leave the scene almost instantly.

And days before that, three Myrtle Beach women told police that their vehicle had been stopped and they'd been abducted by strange difficult-to-describe creatures in a UFO. Under hypnosis, each of the women told the same story. And under scrutiny by a polygraph, they continued to appear to be telling the truth.

The Ocean Herald will continue to report on these and related stories about unidentified flying phenomena. Readers are encouraged to contact the newspaper and police if they witness anything strange in the sky.

It took me about two hours to write this story, which, again, almost seemed to write itself.

A few hours later, the story appeared online and on the front page, below the fold, with the headline:

Grave digger reports UFO sighting at local cemetery; says strange orange ball of light tampered with a freshly dug burial site

The secondary deck below the headline was:

Husband of woman buried in grave fears his wife's corpse may have been stolen; seeks court- ordered exhumation

Boxed in with the story and headline was a sketch, by the newspaper's graphic artist, of a circular-shaped disc-like craft hovering over a tombstone.

* * *

Looking forward to some quiet, restful time at the beach after such a stressful previous 24 hours, I got home and changed into shorts, athletic shoes, a tee shirt, and my favorite Myrtle Beach Pelicans ballcap.

Nothing like a stroll next to the waves, seagulls, dunes, and in the salt air to clear your head and reset your soul. Today the ocean was especially beautiful, more green than blue with a few fishing boats in the distance.

I picked up a few broken shells, like I always do, and stuffed them into a pocket. One of these days, I figured I'd make something out of the thousands of shells I'd already collected. Or I'd give 'em to some landlocked person who had no idea what it was like to live near the ocean.

And that's when I noticed I had a voicemail.

Why my iPhone hadn't rung I'll never know, but such is life.

I turned up the volume and pressed play:

"Mr. Harmless, you don't know me but that don't make no difference. I damned well know you and I know your scummy kind."

Deep breathing and a pause of a few seconds from his end of the line.

And then the message resumed—a bit louder and with a nastier tone.

213

"You're nothin' but a blood suckin', sneakin', lyin', betrayin' son of a bitch yella journalist!

"Don't think for a second that nobidy saw ya writin' down ever' word at our church prayer meetin'. And you with your fancy, dancy phone recordin' us.

"Not even askin' for our permission and not tellin' a soul who you were.

"Just waltzing right inta our house a' worship and pretendin' that the Lord sent ya to be with us.

"But you didn't fool me for a pea pickin' minute. I knowed you wuz a spy when I first laid eyes on ya.

"So let this be fair warnin' to you and your kind. Don't you ever even think about settin' foot back in our church! Cause we'll be watchin' for ya and you don't EVEN want ta know what we'd do to ya. Good-bye and Amen!"

I looked for a number where the call originated and there was none. He'd evidently blocked his number.

I saved the voicemail to forward to my editor, sure. If nothing else, he'd get a kick out of it.

Chapter 20
Coverup At The Airport

I tried for the next few days not to dwell on the threatening voicemail from Mr. Anonymous Churchgoer, instead focusing on a note that I had somehow forgotten about.

I had almost thrown it away, but there it was, crumpled and squeezed into a compartment of my wallet. I wouldn't have noticed it had I not been looking for my voter registration card.

So, the classic case of serendipity.

The note was from the young intern who had nervously squeezed it into my hand at the last second after I exited the elevator at the airport.

It included her name, Jessica Perry, and her cell number.

And that was it. No kind of urgent message or desperate appeal for me to write a certain kind of story about a particular topic.

And it had no romantic overtures, unfortunately for me, because the young woman was extremely cute.

Well, then, why not give her a call?

Which I did at that very moment.

She answered on the second ring, instantly recognizing my voice and clearly remembering me.

But she wouldn't go into what was on her mind—at least not on the phone.

Preferring instead to meet me at a popular bagel and coffee shop not far from where I lived.

About one hour later, we met up, shook hands, and sat at an outside small round table.

I ordered a black coffee and toasted cinnamon-raisin bagel with cream cheese. Jessica said she wanted a bowl of fruit and a glass of organic vegetable juice.

Figures, I thought. *That's how she stays looking so fit and trim.*

It was an understatement to say she had a nice figure.

No, she had a stunning one.

Jessica, who I soon learned was a graduate student in aviation science at Coastal Carolina University, was maybe an inch or two shorter than me, had long shiny blond hair that cascaded onto her chest, the prettiest blue eyes I'd ever seen, and a face that seemed to be made for the movies.

And her body? Well, let's just say I'm sure it turned many a man's head.

And not that her clothes were particularly revealing, but her short skirt and matching sleeveless blouse, showing just a hint of cleavage, kept my attention.

As she began talking, I had a tough time focusing on her words. I wouldn't say I was drooling but I must have been close because she asked me a couple of times if I followed what she was saying.

I got the feeling that this had happened to her before so I tried harder to stay focused on what she was saying.

217

But it was still incredibly hard not to get lost in her eyes.

She had started the conversation with a pointed question:

"Lester, do you believe in extraterrestrials or UFOs?"

When I hesitated to answer, she repeated her question:

"I asked you, Lester, whether you believe in extraterrestrials or UFOs? It's a simple question. Do you or don't you?

I responded that I really didn't know what to believe or not believe. But that I had been trained throughout my short career in journalism to be skeptical of just about everything, let alone wild, far-fetched claims. Most people, it had been my experience, simply believed what the majority thought was factual, and that wasn't really the way I patterned my life or my own belief system.

Which must have been a reasonable answer for her because she took another sip of her juice, smiled, and put one of her hands—soft and sensuous, by the way—into my right hand.

"I took you for an honest, straight-arrow fellow when I noticed you talking to the controllers in the tower at the airport," she said. "So that's a big reason I'm trusting you."

"Trusting me with what?"

"With what I'm about to share with you concerning what's going on with the radar at the airport?"

"And what would that be, exactly," I wondered aloud to her.

"Before I tell you, you have to promise me that you'll never tell where you got this information. Are we clear about that? Do you promise? And if a journalist makes a promise, isn't that something that no one can ever make him reveal?"

"It's sort of like that, Jessica. Let's just say that you have my word, my promise that I won't tie what you're about to tell me to you."

"And no one can ever make you break your promise. Correct, Lester?" she asked me.

"A promise is a promise, Jessica. But courts or judges in some extreme instances have ordered journalists to break their promise to reveal a

219

source, and if they haven't done that, some of them have been sentenced to jail."

"But why would a judge throw a journalist in jail? Wouldn't that be against the law?" she asked.

I explained to her that in some rare circumstances, when a person's life or freedom was at stake, the journalist had to obey the law. And if law enforcement or a prosecutor couldn't determine the source of a certain piece of valuable information, some reporters had been jailed for not naming their source.

But that was very rare, I added, because judges, courts, or other authority figures hated attacking the First Amendment to the Constitution.

Which upheld freedom of speech and freedom of the press in America.

And was a solid protection for journalists not to have to spill their guts in front of a judge.

But then again, you never say never, meaning no protection for journalists was ever absolute in every situation.

She got silent and I could tell she was weighing her options: to trust or not trust me.

Then she took a deep breath and I sensed she was about to confide in me.

"But first, I have a few questions for you," she said teasingly.

"Questions about what?"

"Well, if you have to know, they're all about space travel?"

"You can ask but don't hold your breath that I'll have even the slightest inkling of what you're talking about. But go ahead and ask me."

I said a silent prayer that I wouldn't seem overly dumb.

She laughed and said again that she had sized me up correctly from the get-go— that I was a straight arrow, down to earth honest man.

"First question, Lester. What is Oumuamua?"

"No idea."

She spelled it for me and said it was pronounced au moo uh moo uh.

"Still no idea," I said.

"Second question: Define a black hole in outer space."

"Something that has to do with what's happening in another galaxy?" I guessed.

"Third question: What is dark energy?"

"Again, no idea, Jessica."

"Fourth and last question: In what year did the famous UFO incident in Roswell, New Mexico, occur?"

"That one I do know, because I've researched it—1947."

"Excellent!" she said. "Well, you got one out of four—not exactly off the charts for a guy who's been writing about extraterrestrials and flying saucers, but you did know about Roswell. So that's a start."

"I've got one for you, Jessica," I said. "It's not a question. More like a situation. I'd like your take on it."

She took a sip of her drink and nodded for me to continue.

"It's like this," I said. "A car ran over a boy's dog and killed it. And the kid was devastated. So the boy's family, trying to console him, placed a pink cross, along with flowers, alongside the road where the car hit the dog. They also sprinkled the dog's ashes around the flowers.

"You follow me so far, Jessica?"

She nodded again; her eyes locked on mine.

"Well, wouldn't you know that someone came along the other day and pulled up the cross and flowers? So now there's nothing there on that spot at all. Nothing to mark where the dog died. And the little boy is crushed. He doesn't understand how someone could be so cruel. His parents have tried to explain to him that there are mean, bad people in this world. But their son still doesn't understand how someone could be so uncaring.

"And now I have to write about this."

Jessica's eyes seemed to have moistened as I told her the story.

She dabbed them with a napkin.

"And you're asking me what exactly?"

"I'm not asking you anything, just trying to give you a sense of what I'm confronted with almost every day. Maybe subconsciously trying to defend myself for being so ignorant about outer space and black holes and that sort of thing. Truth to tell, I'm pretty much consumed with writing about everyday stuff like a little boy's dead dog's cross being stolen. Or about a young married couple having sex, in broad daylight, on the Myrtle Beach skywheel, and being charged with indecent exposure.

"So that doesn't leave me much time to get up to speed about extraterrestrials or exoplanets or black holes or whatever. No excuse, I know, but I'm just forever up against a deadline. The news, or whatever you want to call it, never stops. And I have to write about it."

Jessica said nothing but I could tell that she understood.

Maybe, I thought, *if I'm lucky, she'll cut me some slack on all this extraterrestrial stuff and we can at least be friends.*

I gently reminded her that she had wanted to meet with me to tell me something she'd rather not share on the phone.

She squirmed uneasily.

"If you breathe a word of what I'm about to tell you, Lester, I'll lose my internship. So I shouldn't even be talking to you. But for some reason, I trust you, so here goes.

"We have something at the airport called ASR. That stands for Airport Surveillance Radar, and it's fairly powerful in what it can detect."

"Just how powerful are we talking about, Jessica?"

"It can pick up any object up to 25,000 feet high, within about a 60-mile radius of the airport. So it's a key part of our main air traffic control system. It lets us know what's out there up in the sky, what's inbound, and what's outbound. And it even communicates, via radio signals, with the transponders of aircrafts. Transponders tell us an aircraft's identification, its altitude, and speed. All

225

that data comes up on the radar screen in the operations room at our airport tower and we monitor it constantly. It's all part of a system called Terminal Radar Approach Control—or TRACON.

"What I'm trying to tell you is that without TRACON, we'd never be able to see to it that the air traffic in and around Myrtle Beach International Airport was flowing safely, with correct aircraft separation so as to avoid midair collisions."

I told her I thought I had the general idea—that radar and transponders were essential tools of air traffic control, along with good clear communication between the airport tower and the pilot.

But I wondered what she was leading up to.

And so she finally spilled it.

"We're getting a lot of blips, just about every day, on the radar screen in the operations room that we can't identify," she said, lowering her voice. "And they're not the kind of blips that any of us in the tower have ever seen before. It's like they're, well..."

Her voice trailed off.

"Like what, Jessica? Finish your thought."

Again, she chose her words carefully.

'They don't behave like jets or propeller-driven aircraft or helicopters. For a few seconds they're on the screen, maybe 40 miles from the airport, and next thing ya know they're almost on top of us, directly above the tower. But they're only there for, like, milliseconds. Then they zoom off faster than lightning, it seems.

"No one, even the guys that've been working in air traffic control for more than 20 years, has ever seen anything like them. It's just the weirdest, strangest, aerial phenomena you can imagine. So bizarre and mysterious that the director—my boss, Mr. Staley—dismisses the blips as anomalies of the radar.

"He's usually on top of it with four feet if there's an aircraft inbound to the airport that's unidentified. Especially if it's a high-speed unknown object, he almost loses his mind. But with these mysterious blips, it's like he's in denial."

"So what has he said to the rest of his workers in the aircraft control tower?"

Jessica didn't say anything for a few seconds, but then she spoke.

"Just that our radar system is old and needs updating and maybe even replacing and that we can't trust it any longer. And not to say a thing about this to anyone. And if we do, it could be our job."

I asked her why all the secrecy.

She responded that she had no idea. And that possibly he feared what might happen should the existence of the unidentified, mysterious radar blips become public knowledge.

"Meaning what, exactly, might happen that would be so terrible?" I asked her.

"You know what I'm saying," she said. "Ratcheting up the hysteria already bubbling under the surface about flying saucers over Myrtle Beach. A sense of panic or fear or dread—whatever you want to call it. The whole idea that visitors from outer space, or from God knows where, have decided to descend on our community.

"Not to mention that he'd have to answer to the public—AGAIN—about not asking the Air Force to scramble jets to identify whatever it is that our radar is detecting."

My immediate response was anger.

Anger that the person in charge of air traffic control at Myrtle Beach International Airport was endangering the safety of hundreds of thousands of people.

People who depended on him and his team of workers to keep the skies safe, as well as all aircraft in our area taking off and landing on schedule and flying at the altitude and speed assigned to them.

In other words, jets, planes, helicopters, and any other flying objects doing what they are supposed to do, per their flight plans, and what they're told to do by air traffic controllers.

My prediction: the newspaper would soon be embroiled in another controversy with Mr. Ted Staley, director of the air traffic control tower at our airport.

No way that could be avoided.

I looked forward to it.

Jessica and I said our good-byes and promised to stay in touch. While a farewell hug would have been nice, none was offered and I didn't press it, hoping there'd be a hug or something even more intimate at some point in the future.

And I assured her again that I'd honor my promise to her.

Which would be difficult, given her explosive revelation about the mysterious radar blips.

Chapter 21
Peeling Back The Onion

Before I'd even had a chance to consult with my editor about what appeared to be a potentially dangerous coverup at the airport, I got a call from Maxine Robinson.

She asked if I'd be interested in having, as she called it, a "sit-down eyeball to eyeball interview" with her about her encounter with the flying saucer.

Which took me by surprise because I had been under the impression that she only granted interviews for a price.

I of course jumped at the chance to speak with her and asked if her two friends and fellow "abductees," Lucille Mulligan and Ida Mae James, would be joining us.

Not this time, she replied.

She explained that they had given her permission to deal with the press on their behalf.

So we set it up for me to meet her for a recorded interview that afternoon at 3 at a picnic shelter at Myrtle Beach State Park.

Just the two of us, and we agreed there'd be no constraints on what I'd ask her.

Three o'clock couldn't come soon enough. I had been eagerly wanting to speak with Maxine or the other two for the last several weeks but had no success.

For one thing, Maxine and Ida Mae had been on an extended trip—including appearing as guest speakers at a national MUFON (Mutual UFO Network) conference in Las Vegas. They'd also made the rounds on the UFO speaking circuit in Denver, San Diego, Portland, Boise, and, not surprisingly at the granddaddy of UFO conferences in (where else?) Roswell, New Mexico.

Wherever Maxine and Ida Mae went, they'd been paid well and their expenses—airfare, hotels, meals, car rentals—had been covered in their entirety.

In short, the two women had made the most of a good thing, or, depending on your point of view, a traumatic thing.

Not so, however, with their other friend, Lucille Milligan—the third "abductee."

She had become extremely reclusive. Had not left her house since the night of the encounter. Wouldn't even answer her phone. Wanted nothing to do with any fanfare associated with coming in contact with aliens. Shied away from the public.

In short, was incommunicado. Had retreated to her own cocoon and wished never to be bothered or asked about her reported UFO experience.

* * *

I arrived at the appointed rendezvous location— the picnic shelter—at 2:45 p.m. and Maxine was already there.

She was tanned and wore dark glasses with a straw, wide-rimmed sunbonnet. But the hat didn't hide the few freckles on her nose and chin. A simple pink skirt, with seashells embroidered on it, and a plain white short-sleeved blouse completed her outfit. She was barefoot, having apparently removed her sandals before I got there to take a short stroll on the beach.

"Great choice of location for us to chat!" she beamed. "In fact, I love Myrtle Beach State Park. It's like driving through a thick maritime forest when you come in here. I never get tired of the park, the woods, or this beach. For sure, it's one of my favorite places on the Grand Strand."

I told her I couldn't agree more and that I came here often just to clear my head and breathe in the salt air coming off the ocean.

And then we got down to business. Me asking her anything I could think of related to the police report I'd read weeks ago describing what had happened to the three women on that fateful evening. And she, in turn, answering my questions—sometimes at length, other times with just a few words, depending on how much she wanted to reveal or perhaps was able to reveal, based on her recollection of the event.

We sat there and spoke for going on three hours— the roaring, crashing waves in the background, the wind whipping off the ocean and keeping us cool, and the seagulls flapping their wings in the breeze and cawing loudly.

About halfway through, we took a 15-minute restroom and drink break, which was good, because in-depth, interviewing saps your energy.

At last, when we wrapped it up, I thanked her and promised I'd do my best to represent what she shared with me as accurately as possible.

"Because that's what you always do as journalists, ain't that right?" she said, smiling.

"And the only thing I'll change is a word here and there to make things more clear or grammatically correct—with your permission, of course," I said.

She grinned again. "I trust you, Lester Harmless. Why I do, I'm not sure. But I just got a good feelin' about ya in the first few minutes we met. I'm knowin' you'll do me right."

That evening, I began transcribing the interview. Because I couldn't wait to get Maxine's words down on paper. Besides, it would make writing the story the next day that much easier. Which I did and which got front page priority along with a photo of Lucille, Ida Mae, and Maxine provided by the latter.

Here's what appeared in the newspaper and on the paper's website:

One local woman's recollection of what it was like to be abducted a few weeks ago by what she says were creatures from another world

Maxine Robinson shares her story with the Ocean Herald

By Lester Harmless
General Assignment Reporter
The Ocean Herald

Three weeks ago, three Myrtle Beach residents—Lucille Mulligan, Maxine Robinson, and Ida Mae Jones—reported to police that they had been taken up into a huge disc-shaped, glowing object and examined by creatures from outer space.

This is the account of one of those women, Maxine Robinson, who told this newspaper this week that she has been authorized by Lucille and Ida Mae to publicly share what happened in their UFO encounter.

What follows is an exclusive interview with Ms. Robinson who spoke yesterday with me for three hours.

These are edited excerpts from this reporter's conversation with Ms. Robinson. Only slight edits were made for conciseness and clarity.

Have you been approached by many journalists—or by others—asking you to share your story about the UFO?

Yes, of course. It seems that from the day we filed that police report about what happened to the three of us—me, Ida Mae, and Lucille—our phones have been ringing off the hook, people have been knocking on our doors and, well, you get the idea. Everybidy wants ta know when it happened, where it happened, how it happened, and what specifically those things did to us. You can't imagine the amount of attention we've gotten and it's still goin' on.

When someone gets in touch with you wanting you to talk to them about the UFO event, is there some part of you that says, 'Oh no! Not again!' Does it ever get old telling and retelling your story?

You know, to be honest, maybe it does get a bit tiring, but at the same time I know the public's intensely interested in what happened to us. Especially that thing bein' from another world and all. And if somebidy is willin' to listen, I'm willin' to talk. That's just the kinda person I am.

So, with that being said, tell me, in your own words what happened that night to you and your two friends, Ida Mae and Lucille.

Well, here goes. We were on our way back home to Myrtle Beach from a barbecue restaurant in Loris. It's our favorite place to celebrate special occasions. And this particular day bein' Lucille's birthday, me and Ida Mae decided to treat her to dinner, along with a birthday cake that I'd baked for her.

So, we'd had a good time at the restaurant and were on our way home in my old car on a back road between Loris and Myrtle Beach. I remember it bein' a full moon and the night just packed with twinklin' stars. I know that cause I'd glanced up at the sky as we got'n the car to head home. We'd had a really great time celebratin' her birthday dinner with her.

And so the three of you were on your way home, I take it. Who was driving and then what happened?

I happened to be behind the wheel. Ida Mae sat up front with me. And Lucille was in the back seat.

238

Before you continue, I have to ask you a question. Did any of you have any alcoholic beverages that night?

None of us drank anything alcoholic. I had sweet tea. I think Ida Mae and Lucille each had Coca-Cola™.

Okay. So you're driving home. Then what happened?

Nothing out of the ordinary at first. Just the usual bumps in the road and I remember having to swerve to avoid hitting a dog. Another thing I recall is seeing a South Carolina state trooper pulled off on the side of the road, shielded by a few trees—like he didn't want to be noticed, but I sure enough spotted him and made sure I was drivin' the speed limit.

And then, a few miles later on down the highway, was when I first noticed somethin' wasn't just right.

What do you mean?

It wasn't anything I saw. But rather our car. I hadn't slowed down but yet the car was going much slower, like the tires were bein' held back somehow. Like the car was just barely ploddin' along instead of rollin' at 55 miles per hour. Ida Mae asked me why I was goin' so slow all of a sudden. That's

239

when I glanced down at the speedometer.
I was shocked!

So what did the speedometer say?

It didn't say nothin'. The needle
didn't point to a certain number.
Instead, it was just going back and
forth—from zero to one-hundred miles an
hour. But we sure weren't goin' no
hundred miles per hour, I know that. We
were just creepin'. And then our lights
started flashin' on 'n' off and even
the light inside the car would come on,
then flicker off. And the radio started
actin' crazy. I'd had it tuned to a
Beatles station. We'd been hummin'
Beatles' songs all night long, and then
it just switched to classical symphony
music. Damnedest thing I ever heard!

So what happened next?

Well, about this time, Ida Mae asked me
what the heck was goin' on. Lucille,
well, she acted shell shocked. Didn't
say nary a word. And so I stopped the
car, right there in the middle of the
road, and we all got out. And that's
when we saw the damnedest sight I ever
saw in my life.

Saw what exactly?

A flyin' saucer as big as a barn. I
mean, that thing was huge and then
some! It was spinnin' and bright orange

and all of a sudden it shined a light
down on us, and we couldn't move an
inch. We were helpless. I guess
'immobilized' is the word I've heard to
describe it. I looked at Ida Mae and
she was orange. And so was Lucille. And
I guess I was, too. That's when I got
scared. Real scared.

And before you know it, whatever that
thing was—a flyin' saucer or a
spaceship from another planet or
whatever—we were all inside of it.
Don't ask me how that happened cause I
don't know. But we were lying on our
backs on a table and then we saw the
creatures. They were starin' right
through us, like their eyes could kill
us if they'd a wanted ta do that.

But they didn't hurt us at all. Just
scared the daylights outta us. Ran some
kind of wand over our entire bodies
like they were lookin' down into our
bones and organs. And did I mention we
was nekkid? Yep, nekkid as jaybirds.
They undressed us sure as I'm sittin'
here with you. And shortly after that
they put our clothes back on us. And
through the whole process, they weren't
makin' a sound. Not so much as a peep.
Just quiet, silent, weird creatures
from another world—examinin' us, I
guess.

Can you describe them?

I think I counted three of them, but
Ida Mae says she saw four of 'em. Best
way I can put it is they didn't look
like anything from this planet earth.
They had long spidery lookin' legs and
skinny arms and just little slits for
eyes and no nose or mouth that I could
see. Just strange beyond your wildest
dreams. What they wasn't was little
green men. In fact, they had no color
at all. Might have even been close to
transparent, but not quite, the more I
think about it. I'll never forget 'em.
That's for sure.

So how long were you on that table?

Everybody asks us that and we really
don't have a good answer, because we
lost all sense of time. But just a wild
guess would be about 15 minutes. And
then, lo and behold, we found ourselves
back in our car—as if nothin' had ever
happened. But it did happen. We all
agree on that. And then we had ta
decide if we'd tell anybody about it.
Lucille wanted us to stay silent. But
Ida Mae and me—well, I wouldn't be here
talkin' to ya if Lucille had had her
way. The rest, as they say, is history,
except that no way is this thing that
happened to us over yet. Because some
of it's still havin' an effect on us.

**What do you mean by that—that it's
still having an effect on you?**

I mean that no matter how many times we
tell our story, there's them that will
never believe us. And that hurts us to
the core.

**But under hypnosis, you, Ida Mae and
Lucille have told essentially the same
story about the UFO encounter. And all
three of you have also passed a
polygraph test, which has concluded,
with a high degree of confidence, that
the three of you are telling the truth.
And yet you say a good many skeptics
still feel strongly that you are lying?**

Well, let's end on this note: there's
liars and there's lyin' liars, and then
there's folks that're tellin' the
truth. And that's what me and my two
friends are doin'—tellin' the
unvarnished truth. But some people
ain't never goin' to accept that cause
they think UFO's are a fraud hoisted on
the public. That they're a part of
science fiction.

**One last question. What do you say to
those who have accused you of making
the whole thing up just so people would
pay you for your story?**

I say I wouldn't go through again what
happened to us that night for ten

million dollars! And by the way, you can tell 'em what you're payin' me for this interview. Last I heard, it was exactly nothin'.

Chapter 22
Drama In The District Judge's Courtroom

Randolph Dickinson hadn't given up on his fervent quest to have his late wife's body exhumed from her resting place at Pleasant Grove Cemetery.

Not by a long shot.

In fact, he'd hired a lawyer, at $400 an hour, to fight for the exhumation in Horry County District Court.

The court date had finally arrived, with District Judge Marilyn P. Stuart expected to render a decision expeditiously.

Judge Stuart had already carefully reviewed the petitions—for exhumation and against it—but she still said she would consider hearing limited oral testimony from the two attorneys and maybe, if time allowed, from one or two others. So she had set aside time in her oak-paneled courtroom in Conway, the county seat of Horry County, to hear from both sides. That was to commence at 9 a.m. Monday.

In this case, the witnesses who could potentially be called to testify were Randolph Dickinson; his sister-in-law (and sister of the deceased) Robin Jones; Miles Elliott, the grave digger at the cemetery; and Jefferson Aller, superintendent of the cemetery.

I had done some quick research on the legality of exhumations in South Carolina and found that while they did occur, especially in police investigations, they were quite rare. In even rarer instances, graves had been opened at the repeated requests of family members who had mistakenly forgotten to remove a valuable piece of jewelry from the deceased's body.

However, judges in South Carolina tended to be ultra conservative in their exhumation rulings—with the vast majority siding with the sentiment that gravesites were not to be disturbed.

Unless, that is, a judge could be persuaded that an abundance of evidence justified a disinterment.

Exhumations had been granted, on rare occasion in death penalty cases, to help clear a person's name, or, conversely, to help send a person to prison or to the electric chair.

And with South Carolina just recently approving the firing squad as a method of execution, a forensic examination of a dug-up corpse might result in someone being shot to death—by authority of the state.

I got to the courthouse, a stately old antebellum-looking red brick, two-story building with four giant white columns at the front entrance, at about 8:30.

Towering maple trees and lush green grass lined each side of the wide sidewalk leading up to the front concrete steps.

And there on the huge porch at the front entrance were several men and women. A few held signs that variously said, "Leave Her Resting Place Be" or "Is Nothing Sacred Anymore?" or, the most blunt one, "Ain't No Reason To Dig Her Up!"

I treaded softly, realizing that some of these same folks may well have been at the evening church service I attended not long ago.

One of them for sure remembered me.

"It's him!" he shouted. "That bloodsucker spyin' reporter who broke bread with us and betrayed us!

Get on outta' here!" he commanded. "You got no business at this here court session. Cause the last thing we're needin' taday is a lying, spyin' yella journalist!"

I walked carefully among and through them and placed my right hand on the giant brass handle of the front courthouse door. With my back to them, as I pulled on the handle, I heard someone clear his throat and mount a huge gob of spit which plastered the back of my neck.

Disgusting, for sure, but I knew better than to turn around and engage them.

Inside the expansive, ornate courtroom, a stenographer had seated herself just below and in front of where Her Honor would soon hold sway.

A few people—most likely from the congregation of the Salt and Light Nazarene Church—trickled in and sat in the middle two rows of bystander seats.

Randolph Dickinson sat at the plantiff's table on the right side of the room. With him was an attorney who would be arguing, I figured, on Mr. Dickinson's behalf and in favor of the exhumation. I'd soon learn that his name was Daniel C. Stegeman, Esq.

Seated at the witness table on the left side of the room was Robin Jones, cemetery superintendent Jefferson Aller, and Edgar M. Dale, Esq. their attorney (who would argue against exhuming the body).

About a dozen other people wandered into the courtroom, more out of morbid curiosity than anything else, I figured, and plopped themselves down in the back two rows of cushioned seats.

Two uniformed bailiffs, each carrying sidearms and walkie talkies, positioned themselves at the front and back of the courtroom. One of them had layers of fat sagging over his gunbelt. The other, with a body that could have been chiseled out of granite, looked to be in perfect physical condition.

"All rise," one of them shouted as the Honorable District Judge Marilyn P. Stuart entered the room. She wore a long, flowing black robe with a blue scarf wrapped around the front of her neck. She motioned nonchalantly for everyone to be seated as she sat down in what appeared to be the largest and most comfortable chair in the courtroom behind a massive, curved, finely polished mahogany desk.

Directly behind her, hanging majestically on the wall, was a huge circular black and gold seal. In its middle was an eagle with its wings fully extended. The eagle's talons clutched arrows with pointed tips and some sort of cutting, it appeared, from a tree or other kind of plant (possibly representing peace?). The words "E PLURIBUS UNUM" were near the eagle's beak. And around the eagle, in a gold circle, were the words UNITED STATES DISTRICT COURT and DISTRICT OF SOUTH CAROLINA.

What struck me about the courtroom was its decorum, its air of authority and dignity, its unmistakable aura that this is where, truly, the proverbial rubber met the road with regard to what was legal and what wasn't. This was where dreams were realized—or crushed. Where freedom was gained or people were sentenced to prison. Where fortunes in lawsuits were awarded—or denied. Where lives, regardless of the outcome of the court case, were transformed forever.

Wonder, I thought, *if the late Linda Sue Dickinson, would have imagined in a million years that her death—and then her corpse—would have caused such a stir?*

Nope. She couldn't have even dreamed this, I thought. *But now it's happening, and we will see what we will see.*

Judge Stuart opened the proceedings by cautioning everyone that she wouldn't tolerate outbursts of anger or celebration in her courtroom. She warned that anyone behaving in such a manner would be quickly removed by a bailiff, and, if they persisted in not being able to control their emotions, they would be found in contempt of court and escorted to the county jail.

She then instructed attorney Edgar Dale to begin his opening argument.

Dressed in a pinstriped blue suit, a starched, laundered shirt with a bright red tie and fine leather shoes, Dale rose up, walked eagerly toward the bench and then turned to face the gallery. Behind him and to his left, an American flag, outlined on three sides with gold rayon fringe, stood as if at vigil.

A "tall drink of water," as some old-timers on the Grand Strand had described him, with a sharply protruding chin, angular nose and penetrating dark eyes, Dale said he would be brief and not waste the court's time on what he predicted would be "frivolous, science fiction arguments" advanced by the opposing attorney.

"Your honor," he said, turning suddenly from the gallery of spectators and facing the judge, "this is, if you'll pardon the expression, as simplistic a case as a nailed shut coffin. The family of the deceased, meaning specifically her blood younger sister, respectfully requests that her grave not be disturbed.

"Mrs. Linda Sue Dickinson, who unfortunately died from a tragic accident, was laid to rest in Pleasant Grove Cemetery, and there she was meant to remain, undisturbed, until the Good Lord called her home to eternal Heaven.

"And I would remind your Honor that it's extremely rare in the state of South Carolina that a grave is opened and the remains disinterred. It is usually only done as an absolute last resort, when circumstances warrant, such as in a law enforcement investigation or in a case where the corpse should have been autopsied, but was not, before burial.

"In this case, Linda Sue Dickinson's sole surviving blood relative—her younger sister Robin Jones—

has made it crystal clear that she in no way wants her sister's remains unearthed.

"That same sentiment is echoed by Mrs. Dickinson's beloved church family, members of the Salt and Light Nazarene Church, who say it's abhorrent to bother Mrs. Dickinson's resting place.

"I said I would make my remarks brief, Your Honor, and I'll just close by saying this: gravesites are not meant to be disturbed. Coffins and corpses, once placed into the ground, are meant to remain there—never, except in the most compelling circumstances, to be dug up.

"And they are certainly not meant to be dug up as a result of some absurdly fantastical story involving little green creatures in a flying saucer that somehow penetrated the grave and tampered with the dead. THAT'S THE MOST PREPOSTEROUS STORY I'VE EVER HEARD IN MY WHOLE LIFE! So I respectfully ask Your Honor to please respect the wishes of Robin Jones and her church family. Leave Mrs. Dickinson's final resting place alone.

"Oh, and one more thing, Your Honor. I won't waste this court's time by calling him as a witness because you already have in your possession the sworn statement of Mr. Jefferson Aller, superintendent of Pleasant Grove Cemetery. He is adamantly opposed to the state of South Carolina, meaning this court, issuing an order of exhumation for Mrs. Dickinson's remains. And this from a professional who has worked in the cemetery business for going on 30 years. You will read, if you haven't already done so, that Mr. Aller, in all his years of service, has been involved in less than a dozen exhumations—all of them resulting from law enforcement petitions that were approved by a duly appointed or elected judge. Certainly not a single one of the exhumations stemmed from a report of a UFO tampering with a buried human being. I rest my case, Your Honor."

"Thank you, Mr. Dale," Judge Stuart said. "Mr. Stegeman, are you ready to present your case in favor of exhuming the body?"

"I am, Your Honor, and I only have one request," Stegeman replied.

"And what is that, Mr. Stegeman?"

"That this court will keep an open mind about what I'm about to say. And that the court will not dismiss as impossible or fiction the idea that beings from another world have recently visited our community."

Judge Stuart didn't flinch or show any reaction at all to the attorney's request. Instead, she nodded, signaling for him to proceed with his argument.

I took this as an encouraging sign. At least Her Honor didn't gavel him down or laugh him out of her courtroom.

Stegeman approached the bench, then did an about-face so that those in the gallery could fully appreciate what he was about to present.

A short man with a bald head, thick eyebrows, bigger ears than normal, and arms that seemed too long for his torso, he walked with a bit of a limp. He leaned on a cane as he addressed the courtroom.

"Your Honor, I haven't come here to shock you, scare you, or to try to get you to change your core belief system. But something truly amazing and strange has been happening lately in our neck of the woods. Some would even call it unbelievable, logic-defying, astounding.

"I'm referring, of course, to the recent spate of UFO sightings in Myrtle Beach that have been reported by many reliable witnesses. These sightings have been documented in police incident reports, and our local news media, both electronic and print, have focused on them.

"In short, Your Honor, we have been visited by unidentified flying objects—better known as UFOs. That is NOT fiction. It is very much REALITY. Where the UFOs are coming from or who is in them is an open question, but they ARE HERE. There's no disputing that."

At this point, the judge, who I thought had indicated she'd remain open minded and impartial—seemed to be growing impatient.

"Counselor," she said sternly, "we aren't here today to have you lecture us on whether or not UFOs exist. I'll remind you that the matter before this court is whether to issue an exhumation order for a corpse now interred at Pleasant Grove Cemetery. Nothing more and nothing less. Please make your point."

"Yes, Your Honor. My point is that a sworn witness has told police that he personally saw a flying saucer tamper with the gravesite, and possibly with the body, of the late Mrs. Linda Sue Dickinson."

"Objection, Your Honor!" opposing attorney Dale shouted. He rose from his seat and made several gestures of exasperation with his hands and arms.

"On what grounds, Mr. Dale?" the judge, rolling her eyes, asked.

"On the grounds that everything that this so-called sworn witness has said is inadmissible hearsay."

"Your Honor," Stegeman said. "With your permission, I'd like to call that witness to testify. He's seated right now in this courtroom, and you can decide for yourself if he's telling the truth."

Judge Stuart, frowning, rubbed her forehead and took a sip of water from a glass. Then she glanced impatiently at her watch.

"Mr. Stegeman, I'm not sure I'll permit your witness to testify. I already have Mr. Miles Elliott's sworn statement. I know what he's going to say, so what's the point in wasting this court's valuable time?"

"You ain't a bit smarter than me, and I've been sittin' here listenin' to ya run your mouth all mornin'," a hump-backed man protested from the back of the courtroom. Loud enough that the two bailiffs suddenly turned and faced him.

"You a sittin' up there all high an' mighty in your big black robe, thinkin' you ain't havin' to answer to nobidy!"

The judge, taken aback, pointed to Stegeman.

"Mr. Stegeman, is that Mr. Miles Elliott, your witness with the sworn statement?"

"He is, Your Honor."

"Bailiff, remove Mr. Elliott from the courtroom," the judge, pounding her gavel, angrily declared.

One of the bailiffs immediately grabbed the gravedigger and ushered him to the exit.

"Ain't you a wide glide!" Elliott yelled as the obese, jowly bailiff walked him to the door.

With the gravedigger out of the courtroom, Stegeman turned to the judge and apologized for what he had hoped would be a compelling statement from his star witness.

"It's my fault, Your Honor, that Mr. Elliott didn't behave himself in a manner consistent with the decorum of the court. But you do, as you say, have his statement, and I ask that it be entered into the court record for your consideration."

"Granted, Mr. Stegeman."

The judge then turned to attorney Dale and asked if he had anything further to add.

He said he didn't, and the judge started to get up from her seat.

"Wait, please, Your Honor! May I please be granted the opportunity to speak?"

The judge remained seated as Randolph Dickinson asked out loud if he could approach the bench. He said that he was the husband of the woman laid to rest at Pleasant Grove Cemetery.

"Mr. Stegeman, were you aware that the husband of the deceased Mrs. Dickinson wanted to testify?"

"I knew about it, Your Honor, but was under the impression, for the sake of expediting this case, that you were not inclined to hear from witnesses."

"Very well, Mr. Stegeman. But I'll allow this one person to speak."

"Not fair, Your Honor!" Robin Jones objected.

"Bailiff, take that woman out of this courtroom at once and remind her about who is in charge of this proceeding," the judge growled. "And if you can't talk sense into her, see to it that she is not allowed to re-enter."

As the bailiff corralled Robin Jones, kicking and screaming and thrashing about in defiance, Randolph Dickinson approached the chair at the witness stand.

After placing his right hand on a Bible and swearing to tell the truth, the whole truth, and nothing but the truth, Dickinson took his seat.

He told of speaking to the gravedigger and coming away from that conversation with one giant nagging concern. That being the deep fear that his wife's body was no longer in the place where it had been buried.

Or, possibly even worse, that her corpse had somehow been "violated" by aliens from another world.

That sparked a rebuttal from the opposing attorney, Mr. Dale.

"When you say your wife's corpse may have been 'violated,'" Mr. Dale said, "what exactly are you suggesting?"

"That she may have been taken out of the grave by creatures from outer space who removed her from her burial clothes and then did God-only-knows-what to her."

Stretching, yawning, and taking another sip of water, the judge said, "And then, after all that, replaced her fully clothed in her coffin, Mr. Dickinson? Are you also saying that?"

Seemingly struggling for words at that juncture, Dickinson just nodded.

"Am I to take that as a yes on your part, Mr. Dickinson?" the judge asked. "Please answer clearly for the record."

"Yes Ma'am, Your Honor," Dickinson said. "I'm not sure what they would have done to her body, but yes, it's entirely possible they could have undressed her, had their way with her, and then put her back in her clothes."

The judge suppressed a hint of a grin, then said, "So, even if we opened her grave, and she were still lying there in her coffin, you wouldn't be convinced that she had not been violated. Is that correct, Mr. Dickinson?"

Stammering and shuffling uncomfortably on the witness stand, Dickinson managed to grunt, "I guess so, Your Honor. How could I ever be 100 percent sure, given how powerful folks say these aliens are?"

"So, if I understand you correctly, Mr. Dickinson, this court could issue an order of exhumation, which is only to be warranted in the most extreme or pressing circumstances, the grave, at much expense and considerable trouble, could be opened, the casket removed and a forensic exam conducted on the body even if there were absolutely no obvious signs that the body had been tampered with in any way? Do I have that right, Mr. Dickinson?"

"Well, if you put it that way, Your Honor, it seems what I'm asking for is unwarranted. But it IS warranted. Because, again, I don't even know if my wife is still buried there. That's all I have left of her. It's the last place on this earth that I touched her or spoke to her. I wept over her corpse before they closed the lid on her coffin. And I made a promise then that I'd return to her gravesite at least twice a week and talk to her.

"And now, just to think she may no longer even be there."

"SHE'S IN THE GROUND THERE AND YOU DAMN WELL KNOW IT, SO WHY DON'T YOU JUST BUTT OUT AND LEAVE HER BE?! AIN'T NO CALL DIGGIN' UP ALL THEM CANKER WORMS AND SUCH AND DISTURBIN' HER BONES JUST BECAUSE YOU HEARD A LIE ABOUT A FRICKIN' FLYIN' SAUCER!"

That outburst came from a short, squat, stern-faced woman, one of the deceased's close church friends. She had been sitting about midway between the front and back of the courtroom, and, up to this point, no one had even noticed her.

When the angry churchgoer continued ranting on about the utter stupidity of those who believed in aliens and UFOs, the judge would have no more of it. She had the woman removed from the courtroom, instructed the witness seated on the stand that he was done testifying, and announced that she would render her decision in due time.

With that, the court session was adjourned and everyone filed out of the room.

Except for Robin Jones. She went out of her way to make sure she hadn't missed speaking with me.

"I know who you are and why you're here," she said. "And you've done your level best to scare our entire community with those wild UFO stories. I'll bet you're right proud of yourself. Do you really call yourself a journalist?"

"Just reporting the news and doing my job, Ma'am," I responded.

"And you won't be satisfied, I take it, till you've got the whole state of South Carolina looking up in the skies for big, round, orange spaceships."

"Again, Ma'am, just doing my job."

"And it's got nothin' at all ta do with sellin' a bunch of newspapers? Or with makin' money or gettin' noticed? Ain't that also right?" she asked me derisively.

"I'm a journalist, Ma'am. I don't deal with circulation or advertising."

"You and your newspaper are a crock of you know what! And don't you dare write anything negative about my sister or my church. You got that, Mister?"

Chapter 23

Accessing Airport Radar Records

I hadn't forgotten what airport intern Jessica Perry had told me about the unidentified radar data at Myrtle Beach International Airport.

And the fact that Ted Staley, director of the air traffic control tower, seemed so paranoid about anyone talking about them only heightened my curiosity.

Why that fear of disclosure of what ought to be merely routine information captured by the airport's radar systems?

Why the secrecy?

But I was in an awkward position.

I'd given Jessica my word of honor that I wouldn't tell anyone, least of all the always suspicious Ted Staley about what she'd shared with me.

Because if I did that, she'd likely lose her internship. Staley would take no prisoners when it came to discerning who, in his mind, had betrayed a solemn confidence.

It irritated me that what happens in the airport tower or what's recorded there by the tower's computers STAYS IN THE AIRPORT TOWER, NO EXCEPTIONS.

But this was important. Because it seemed to me that the radar at the Myrtle Beach International Airport was likely at the top of the list of most critical tools for our areas's air traffic control and safety.

Planes and jets were landing and taking off at our airport, at all hours of the day and night. But what if some of them had not filed flight plans or had seemingly come from out of nowhere? And were thus unidentified or even worse—misidentified—and were in the crowded airspace around the airport?

So back to my predicament.

How to honor my promise to Jessica and yet somehow get access to those radar records? Which, if what Jessica said was true, pointed to an air traffic control tower team not doing its job to keep our local skies safe and secure.

I made a few phone calls with reporters in other states and learned that what I wanted—access to the radar records at Myrtle Beach International Airport—was not unprecedented. In those states, the press had been known to file a freedom of information request to access the records.

And that certainly seemed like an option for me. Because with the airport at Myrtle Beach being county owned, that is being paid for in full or in part by the taxpayers, that made it a public agency.

And if you were a public agency in South Carolina, that meant you had to abide by the law when it came to disclosure of information to the press or public.

I made a quick close reading of the South Carolina Freedom of Information Act and was heartened.

For unless releasing the requested records breached state or national security or interfered with a law enforcement investigation, the airport had to defer on the side of disclosure.

Which to me meant that I shouldn't have any trouble getting those radar records, for a specific time or date of my choosing, if only I asked for them.

But alas, things are never as simple and smooth as you imagine they'd be.

Even if the law is on your side—which it was in this case.

Because when I emailed Ted Staley and spelled out to him what I wanted from his office—that being an electronic disc copy of the air traffic control radar data for the last 30 days—his response was a big fat, emphatic "NO, YOU CAN'T HAVE THOSE UNDER ANY CIRCUMSTANCE!"

So I reminded him that by not releasing them he'd be violating the state's freedom of information act. Which was akin to pouring the proverbial gasoline on the fire.

"I SAID NO," he replied. "AND I MEANT NO! WHAT IS IT YOU DON'T UNDERSTAND ABOUT ENGLISH?!"

The next day, I emailed him again, explaining that I needed the records for a story I was putting together on local air traffic safety. And that it was my reading of the state's freedom of information act that they were clearly subject to public disclosure.

"You can go to hell with your fishing expedition, Mr. Harmless!" he shot back. "And if you read the state open records law closely, you'll see that there are exceptions to disclosure—such as national or military security. I'm giving you absolutely nothing!"

We exchanged a few more emails, with me pressing him to explain what he meant by the radar records at our local airport having anything to do with national or military security. But I got nowhere. He wasn't budging. He said he didn't have to explain or defend his position and that I needed to BUZZ OFF!

Meanwhile, something interesting on the UFO front was occurring in Washington, D.C. The federal government was just days away from publishing what it promised would be a detailed report about unidentified aerial phenomena. The report had been sparked by public pressure, bordering on outrage, for the U.S. government to finally come clean about what it knew about UFOs.

Public pressure for the report had been ramped up since widespread media coverage of Navy fighter pilots crossing paths with UFOs over the ocean off the coast of San Diego. There'd also been widely publicized UFO encounters involving military pilots off the coast of Virginia Beach, Virginia, and Jacksonville, Florida. What made these encounters so noteworthy was that reliable witnesses, highly trained Navy and Air Force pilots, had been party to them.

And, of course, there had been Roswell, New Mexico, all those decades ago, where UFO-mania had seemingly left a permanent, tantalizing imprint on the public consciousness. Tantalizing because even to this day there are those who accuse the government of a sinister coverup of the events at Roswell.

So with the U.S. government's comprehensive report on unidentified aerial phenomena close to being made public, some noted elected leaders were finally breaking their silence.

They were speaking for the record on a subject— UFOs— that for many years had been consigned mainly to the realms of science fiction, the absurd, or to the imagination.

One of them was Senator Marco Rubio of Florida, who had just made his position on UFOs clear to a reporter for the respected CBS news program "60 Minutes."

"Anything that enters an airspace that's not supposed to be there is a threat," Rubio said.

And when pressed to give his take on why there had been so many recent reports of unidentified aerial phenomena, he said: "Maybe it has a very simple answer. Maybe it doesn't."

To me, it was as if Rubio was speaking about the radar and air traffic control at Myrtle Beach International Airport.

I remembered Jessica Perry's nervous words:

"We're getting a lot of blips, just about every day, on the radar screen in the operations room that we can't identify. And they're not the kind of blips that any of us in the tower have ever seen before.

They don't behave like jets or propeller-driven aircraft or helicopters. For a few seconds they're on the screen, maybe 40 miles from the airport, and next thing ya know, they're almost on top of us, directly above the tower. But they're only there for, like, milliseconds. Then they zoom off faster than lightning, it seems.

No one, even the guys that've been working in air traffic control for more than 20 years, has ever seen anything like them. It's just the weirdest, strangest, aerial phenomena you can imagine."

As if on cue, my cell phone rang just then.

"Hello, am I speaking to Mr. Lester Harmless, the reporter who's been writing about flying saucers?"

"Speaking."

"I think I have something that you'd be interested in."

"And who might this be, please?" I asked him.

"You don't know me but my name is Danny Lovelace. I've just recently resigned from my job in air traffic control at our airport here in Myrtle Beach. I worked there for 35 years, but before I left, I took something with me—something that they don't know that I have."

I asked him what he had but he declined to tell me, saying he'd rather meet me in person first.

So we decided to meet that afternoon at Warbird Park—near the airport but a large enough venue, with its towering pine trees, memorial markers, and vintage Air Force fighter jets, that we likely wouldn't be noticed by others.

At precisely 3 p.m., as we had agreed, he showed up at the park. He was slender, of medium height and appeared to be in his late 60s or early 70s. He had thinning hair and wore a beach tee shirt, faded jeans, and casual sneakers with no socks. A small camouflage backpack was slung over his left shoulder.

He walked to the bench where I was sitting, extended his right hand and said hello.

"I recognized you from your mugshot in the paper," he said with a smile. "I'm the guy who called you about having taken something with me from the airport."

"Danny Lovelace?"

"The one and only," he said with a grin.

"And you say you worked in air traffic control?"

"I sure did, for 35 years, in fact," he said. "But I had taken all I could stand and said to myself, 'Enough is enough.' Not that I didn't like what I was doing. At first, it was my dream job. I had always dreamed of being a pilot, but my eyes weren't good enough, so air traffic control seemed like the next best thing to being behind the controls of a big jet."

"So what exactly did you do in the tower at the airport?"

"You name it," Lovelace said. "I did it. Whether it was communicating with the pilots of inbound or outbound aircraft, making sure that all the flight plans were in order, monitoring the weather, ensuring that all planes maintained their proper vertical and horizontal separations from each other, monitoring the airport's radar...I could go on and on.

"But one thing I never did was notify the Air Force fighter squadron in Charleston to scramble jets. That's because I didn't have the authority. The one and only person who could do that was our esteemed airport tower director, Ted Staley. I think you might have met him?"

"Yes, he and I crossed paths a few times, I guess you could say," I responded, trying to keep a straight face. "But tell me more about your duties with the radar."

"Well, whadya want to know about radar? I guess I've been around radar for about 45 years, countin' my time workin' as a scope dope in the U.S. Air Force."

"Scope dope?" I asked.

"Yeah, that's what we called airmen assigned to monitor the radar scopes," Lovelace explained. "When I joined the Air Force way back when I was a kid, they said my specialty would be aircraft control and warning—just a fancy name for bein' a scope dope, watchin' blips all day on a screen at a radar site.

"But lookin' back on it, it wasn't that bad. One year I was stationed at Poro Point in the Philippines—at Wallace Air Station. Not a bad gig compared to all those guys who pulled their time in Vietnam. We were right on the coast of the South China Sea, a short walk to a nice beach with blue water, nice waves, and silky white sand. And up the mountain from us was a golf course, eatin' places, night clubs, and whatever else you wanted. And dang, it was cool and nice up there in the mountains!"

I steered the conversation back to his work with radar.

"So what was it like staring at that radar scope day in and day out?"

"Not only days, nights too," he quickly noted. "That's just what we did—at least those of us who had one, two, or three stripes. After a few months, it got to be boring and lonely duty just being tied down with that scope shift after shift. But then again, you felt good about doin' somethin' for your country. American soldiers were dyin' every day in Vietnam. Least I could do was not complain about bein' a scope dope.

"And we always had somethin' to look forward to when we got done pullin' our 12 hour-shift."

"Which was what?"

"The Harbor Lights, a small night club just a jeepney ride from the radar site. You talk about bar girls and cold San Miguel beer and even, on occasion, a live band! The Harbor Lights had it all. It was THE PLACE for a homesick American soldier."

"I understand," I said, although not ever having served in the military, I actually didn't. "But again, back to your time as a scope dope, did you ever see any blips on the radar screen that puzzled or scared you or maybe got you to thinking about UFOs?"

"A few times in the Philippines, but as for my work with the radar at Myrtle Beach International Airport, well..."

His voice trailed off as if he were carefully measuring his words and trying to decide whether to continue speaking.

I gave him a few seconds and said everything was okay, assuring him that what he shared with me would stay with me, and with me only.

And that's when he opened his backpack, placed a computer disc on the bench we were sharing, and slid it carefully toward me.

"This is a record of the radar data at our airport for the last month. Beside each blip on the disc, you'll see a small description of the type of aircraft detected, its speed and altitude, point of origin, and its destination. That's standard information for any aircraft picked up by radar."

"So what's the problem?" I asked.

Again he hesitated before continuing.

Then, he said, "Not all the blips have that accompanying identifying info. Many in fact have nothing resembling that. They are what we call, in air traffic control, unknowns. Either someone failed to file a flight plan or the flight plan somehow got misplaced and didn't make it into our computer system or something else, that we don't know about, happened. The end result was that these were unknowns in the airspace within 50 miles of the airport."

"And your superior in the tower, Ted Staley, was aware of this?"

"Not only aware of it but aggravated by it. Irritated by it. Tormented. Baffled. You can choose any of those words to describe his reaction. But one thing he didn't do was pick up the red phone and ask the Air Force to get involved. Nope. He most definitely didn't do that, even though me and some others of us in the tower screamed that we had no earthly idea what was buzzin' around in our skies.

"Nope. His Highness, Mr. Ted Staley, let us know in no uncertain terms that radar wasn't perfect and that birds—Canadian geese, seagulls, what have you—flying in tight formation could give any radar scope a false reading. And that it'd be an utter waste of taxpayers' money and his precious time to get the Air Force to scramble jets."

"So nothing was done then and nothing is being done now to help secure the airspace around our airport? Is that correct?"

"In my opinion," Lovelace, rubbing the palms of his hands together said, "he's putting hundreds of thousands of people at risk. And if the people flying in and out of Myrtle Beach knew how dangerous it was, they'd think long and hard about gettin' on another jet here."

"And so you're expecting me to take this disc and write about it? To confront your boss and demand an explanation? Or to even go above his head, to his superior, and get their take on the situation? Is that what you want?"

Danny Lovelace gave me a I-can't-believe-you're-asking-me-that look and then reminded me how much he had risked in bringing the disc to me.

"Were they flocks of birds?" he asked. "The Chinese? The Russians? Or could they have been something else—something that's hard for us to imagine? You tell me. You're the enterprising journalist. You've been writing about UFOs. Now you have something tangible in your hands to help you make your case—whatever that might be. I wish you the best."

With that, he bid me farewell and left me sitting there in the park. A warm breeze blew across my face. The wind caressed the pine needles in the giant trees. A few pinecones tumbled to the ground. From above, I heard the honking of a big flock of Canadian geese.

Chapter 24
Following Up On The Radar Records

The next day, two things happened.

The Honorable District Judge Marilyn P. Stuart, not breaking with the conservative tradition of South Carolina law, issued a summary judgment that the grave of Linda Sue Dickinson was not to be disturbed and thus that her body would not be exhumed.

Her ruling meant, in effect, that there would be no jury trial on exhumation. Thus, it mattered not whether the plaintiff, the widower of the late Linda Sue Dickinson, had a reasonable basis to suspect that his wife's grave had been tampered with. The judge's summary judgment, issued without an explanation, ended the case—plain and simple.

Lester Harmless was sure that Robin Jones and others at the Salt & Light Church rejoiced at the judge's ruling. And he was just as sure that those who had pressed for the exhumation, namely Randolph Dickinson, were devastated.

He would write a short story on the summary judgment within a few hours, but for now he had something more urgent on his mind: the electronic disc copy of last month's radar records at Myrtle Beach International Airport.

What to do with the disc which had practically been dumped in his lap? How to interpret it?

He made a quick call to Dr. Henry Evans, professor of astronomy at Coastal Carolina University, asking him to meet with him later that day.

Evans told Harmless to be in his office at 4 p.m. sharp after his last class was over. He said he would make sure to set aside time where no students would interrupt them.

"I imagine this has something to do with the UFOs you've been writing about, doesn't it?" Evans asked.

Harmless told him potentially, "Yes, it did, but he didn't want to speak more about it on the phone."

"Very well, then. See you at 4 o'clock this afternoon."

* * *

"So, you think you have something here that's compelling and that'll help you make your case, I take it," the professor said as he slipped the disc copy of the radar data into his computer. Within an arm's length was a steaming hot cup of coffee. He asked his guest if he wanted a cup but Harmless declined.

As the disc was loading, he asked the reporter about what was on it.

"A copy of the radar records from the air traffic control tower at Myrtle Beach Airport for the last month," Harmless said.

"And what, Sir, am I supposed to be looking for," the professor asked as he nudged his glasses up on his nose and scooted closer to the screen of his desktop computer.

Harmless said that it was his understanding that each radar blip should have been accompanied by identifying data such as altitude, kind of aircraft, speed, origin, and destination.

"But I'm told by the person who gave me this disc, who does not want to be named by the way, that that kind of information is missing for a good many of the radar blips," Harmless said. "I haven't even taken a look at the disc myself, but whadya think, Professor?"

At first, Professor Evans, staring intently at his computer, said nothing. As he looked at the screen and thumbed through the various pages of the blips, he scribbled a few notes on a yellow legal pad.

Then he pronounced his verdict.

"What you have here is intriguing because it's what you DON'T have here that's even more compelling. Many of these blips, as you correctly note, are unknowns. But that doesn't necessarily mean they're from another planet. It could just be that a bunch of forgetful, neglectful pilots forgot to file flight plans. Or that flocks of birds have been detected by the airport's radar. What I'm saying is that there might be a perfectly good reason for the lack of identifying data."

"But you're not ruling out the possibility of extraterrestrial objects, correct, Professor," the reporter shot back.

"I'm not ruling anything in or anything out. Not at this point with only this disc as my so-called evidence."

"So even if I placed this record in the hands of the general of the fighter jet squadron in Charleston, you don't think his blood pressure would shoot up? He wouldn't demand a federal investigation," Harmless asked.

"I don't have the slightest idea," the professor responded. "I don't know the man, have never met him, and could not begin to guess how he'd react. And, of course, then you have the matter of authenticity."

"Meaning what, exactly," Harmless asked.

"Is this disc the real McCoy? And where did you get it? How did it arrive in your hands? How do you know it's not fake? That it wasn't created by somebody with an ax to grind? A disgruntled employee or former employee? Lots of sticky questions come to mind. Are you really willing to go out on a limb for this—all by yourself?

"Is the person who gave you this material willing to sign an affidavit and go on the record that this is authentic?"

Harmless told the professor that he gave his solemn pledge not to reveal the person's identity.

"So you, in effect, obtained this from a kind of Deep Throat source who wants you to take all the heat, and fight the possible legal action, while he stays in the background and out of harm's way? That about the size of it?"

"You've accurately characterized it," said the reporter, seemingly more taken aback by the second.

"Then I'd say you have some critical decisions to make," Professor Evans said. "And at the very least, I'd suggest you take steps to verify the authenticity of what you have here—just to make sure you're not being played for a fool. You can't be too sure about something like this. Or, as the old saying goes: better to be safe than sorry."

The professor ejected the disc from his computer, handed it to the now dejected reporter, and took a sip from his coffee.

About that time, someone rapped on his office door.

"No one's in," Professor Evans yelled. "Come back tomorrow, please! I'm not having office hours now!"

"But you're in your office now, Sir," a familiar young female voice responded. "And I won't be but just a minute."

"Then come in if you must but make it brief."

Professor Evans apologized to Lester Harmless for the interruption, explaining that some of his students didn't seem to know the meaning of 'No' or they couldn't read signs he'd posted on his door, or perhaps they just refused to be turned away.

The reporter smiled and said he understood, reminding the professor that it hadn't been that long ago that he himself had been traipsing through the halls of academia.

Jessica Perry, wearing a shirt emblazoned with "Salty Life Forever" and white shorts that accentuated her long-tanned legs, stepped into the office and apologized for interrupting them. She said it was something that absolutely could not wait.

"And what might be so almighty important, young lady?" the professor asked. "And by the way, have you met Lester Harmless, ace reporter at the Ocean Herald?"

She said she had and was even more glad that Harmless was present to hear her news.

"And what might that be, Jessica?"

"There's been another sighting of a big, orange, saucer-like object glowing in the sky over the pier at Myrtle Beach State Park!"

She could scarcely contain her excitement at telling them at least a dozen fishermen had reported seeing the object. And, as they spoke, she said a Myrtle Beach TV station was broadcasting live from the pier interviewing witnesses and trying to paint a picture of what had happened.

As Professor Evans turned on a small color TV set in a corner of his office, Jessica moved to stand next to Harmless so she'd have a better view. The reporter couldn't help but pick up a whiff of her perfume.

"Do you think, Professor Evans, that any of these sightings could have anything to do with the recently discovered so-called odd radio circles in far outer space?

"Or that they could possibly be related to that asteroid that's wider than a hockey rink? You know, the one that astronomers once thought was a sure bet to have collided with our planet?

"Or could the mysterious objects somehow be coming from the dwarf planet Pluto, where just recently we've discovered ice volcanoes on its surface, along with high amounts of nitrogen and methane?"

The professor dismissed all of those guesses as wild speculation, not backed up by any current science. But, that said, he, like his reporter visitor, had struggled to take his eyes off the attractive graduate student. That was just part of Jessica Perry's appeal. She always had that effect on men. In fact, it sometimes was hard to concentrate on what she was saying, given her stunning looks.

The professor turned up the volume on the TV as the camera shot a panoramic view of the ocean and sky at Myrtle Beach State Park.

But no big, bright, orange objects hovering overhead could be seen.

"I'll tell you one thing! It ain't here now but it sure as hell was a few minutes ago. My wife Ethel and I and a lotta others on the pier seen it sure as I'm standin' here talkin' to ya!"

The TV reporter edged the big boom microphone closer to the man's mouth and he willingly obliged.

"It was like nothin' I ever seen in my life! Nothin' at all! And it was spinnin' and darting up and down and sideways and one time it even plunged into the ocean, but then, a few seconds later, it shot right back out quicker'n you can imagine. They ain't nothin' like that our Air Force 'er Navy has. That thing was from another world, plain and simple!"

When the TV journalist asked him to estimate its size, the witness paused for a few seconds.

Then he said, "Close as I could tell, it was as wide as a football field and as long as the parking lot in front of the pier."

"And its sound?"

"It made none. Dead silence as it zipped up and down and sideways."

"That's what scared me the most," said another eyewitness on the pier, an old geezer with big fishhooks in his cap. "It kinda reminded me of a ghost airship—quiet as you please. Nothin' at all like a spacecraft powered by an engine. In fact, I don't think it even had an engine—not the kind

291

that's of this world. Nope. It was powered by something that didn't even leave one iota of evidence of a trail—no smoke, no vapor, no mist, no whatever you wanna call it."

"I take it you've got another UFO story to write," the professor, grinning, said to Harmless. "And at least for this one, you'll have plenty of witnesses to interview. They won't be at any loss for words, for sure.

"And too bad the TV news beat you to the punch."

"They're frequently first but not usually the best at covering an event like this," Harmless said. "TV journalism has a short attention span. It'll fall to us at the paper to give this thing context and perspective."

"Well, in that case, I look forward to reading what you come up with. Keep me posted."

And with that, the professor walked with the reporter and Jessica Perry out of his office.

Amid, by this time, excited chatter in the hallway about the latest UFO sighting.

"Did you hear about the flyin' saucer sighting down at Myrtle Beach State Park?" said one student, his book-filled backpack dangling from his left shoulder.

"Yeah, I did, but nobidy seems to have gotten a picture of the thing in the sky," the student's female companion said. "It's always like that. You'd think at least one of those people fishing on the pier had a cell phone camera. But again, no photographic evidence of what so many people swore they'd seen."

"That's because the aliens know how to evade photography. To them, it's just a primitive technology that's easily nullified," a third student chimed in. "You can take all the pictures you want, but you'll never get a thing when it comes to real honest-to-God UFOs."

Chapter 25
Following Up On The Eyewitnesses

As soon as Lester Harmless left the professor's office, his cell phone rang. It was the newsroom and his instructions were to get down to Myrtle Beach State Park as soon as possible. There'd been multiple reliable sightings of strange balls of orange light in the sky and the Ocean Herald wanted its ace flying saucer reporter on the scene.

"And try your best to get some sort of pictures," an anxious editor pleaded. "You get art and I can promise you we'll flag your story online as Editor's Choice. And when the print edition comes out tomorrow morning, it'll be front and center on page one. But only with art. Remember that!"

Harmless hated to tell Jessica Perry he had to report for work right at that moment because she seemed unusually friendly. And plus she'd been asking him question after question about his job.

"I'm going with you," she said when he informed her he had to cover the UFO sightings at the state park.

It wasn't a question, more of a strident declaration that he wasn't in this alone. That he had a supportive friend who, as a plus, knew quite a bit about the stars, planets, and outer space exploration.

And was extremely cute.

"Well, if you must, Jessica. You're welcome to tag along with me but these things can get boring fairly quickly, especially after I've interviewed the fifth or sixth witness."

She said she didn't mind at all and might even prove to think of something to ask that he hadn't thought of.

So for the rest of that day, they were together at the state park searching out anyone who'd seen the strange flying objects hovering over the ocean. Asking them for their take on what they'd seen. Hoping and praying that at least one of the witnesses had maintained enough composure to snap a picture.

And, lo and behold, one actually had. He happened to be the last man the reporter interviewed.

He had not been fishing from the pier but rather relaxing in his beach chair in the shade away from the bright sunlight, in water about six inches deep beneath the pier.

"That's my favorite hangout at the beach," the 80-year-old retired postal worker said. "Ain't too many other folks underneath there and so I don't have ta worry about some beach umbrella impalin' me. Perfect place just to cool your toes and read and enjoy the waves. But you gotta watch yourself around them pylons. They've got razor-sharp little ocean creatures attached to 'em."

"So how is it that you got a picture of what you saw when so many others, who said they saw the same thing, snapped pictures and got nothing?" Jessica asked the old-timer.

"Ya know, I've been thinkin' about that exact same thing," he replied. "Only thing I can come up with is where I was sittin' when I took my picture. You know, from a distance you can't hardly tell I'm under here, me bein' in the shade an' all. But them other folks, they was out there on the pier or on the beach, clear as day, and whatever they saw...
...Well, let's just put it this way, whatever they saw had to have seen them. But not me. Nope. Not

likely anything seen me sittin' here in this dark spot under the pier."

"And so you're saying that whatever or whoever was in that object over the ocean had some sort of control over being photographed?" the reporter asked.

"Nope. Cause I don't rightly know what we're dealin' with here. But anything's possible. I'll leave it at that."

Lester Harmless and his companion, Jessica, looked at the picture the man had managed to capture on his cell phone. It was sharp, in focus, and compelling. And it was a video to boot!

Compelling because it showed a huge, orange, round ball-shaped object as wide as five houses lined up next to one another just drifting slowly and silently in the sky a few hundred feet above the sea.

And then, as the one-minute video wound down, the object bolted soundlessly far away from the pier and beyond the horizon faster than any flying object Harmless had ever seen.

The old guy sent him the video right there on the spot and said he could use it any way he chose.

"But I ain't lookin' for no fortune er fame. So no need ta pay me anything. But I'll look forward ta readin' your article."

Harmless and Jessica thanked him and said they'd be in touch if anything else came up.

Then they began walking toward the parking lot next to the pier.

And that's where a park ranger asked if they'd had a chance to interview old man Lyle Festus.

"Lyle who?" Harmless asked the officer.

"Festus. That's spelled F E S T U S. When it comes to happenins' in this state park, he doesn't miss a trick. Sees and hears everything, and I do mean everything. He lives in a run-down primitive cabin in the backwoods of the park right up against a swamp. Keeps to himself. Likes it that way. Says he gets along better with gators, turtles, and cottonmouths than he does people. I can take ya there on my four-wheeler if you'd like."

Jessica and the reporter thanked him for the tip and eagerly hopped aboard the off-the-road vehicle with the ranger.

They figured it'd likely be tough going through the wilderness but nothing prepared them for the bumpy, meandering ride through the thick maritime forest that pushed up against the beach.

They were on what appeared to be a semblance of a trail but it was full of roots, overgrown vegetation, briars and jagged rocks. Above and all around them was a dense canopy of wax leaf myrtles, huge live oaks, giant loblolly pines, magnolias, red cedars, hickories, black walnuts, maples, and tulip poplars.

After about two miles of extreme jostling aboard the four-wheeler, the three of them—the park ranger, Jessica Perry, and Lester Harmless—got out of the vehicle and began hiking.

"Far as we can go in my vehicle," the ranger said. "From here on out, you'll have to walk. But it's a short distance to his cabin. Just stay on this path, and whatever's out here that's poisonous'll most likely leave you alone." He pointed to the slightly worn walkway where they all stood. And you'll have to make it back to the parking lot on your own. Duty calls. See ya later." He adjusted his polaroid sunglasses and pulled his cap, with a S.C. state park insignia, snugly down on his head.

Fifteen minutes later, they saw the cabin. But how on earth could a human being survive there? Out here, at least two miles from the beach, deep in the rugged, unforgiving forest? With not another living person to lean on for help or, for that matter, for anything else.

The moss-covered, weathered old cabin itself was an extremely poor excuse for shelter. There was no evidence of electricity or power of any kind, as there weren't any wires going into or out of the structure. There was one step that took you to a rickety old porch, which framed the front door (which, it turned out, was the cabin's only entrance). The place had a cracked brick chimney and one four-paned dirty broken window. In the back of the dilapidated dwelling was an outhouse.

The cabin's most striking feature was that you could barely see it, even at close range. It seemed to be almost entirely encapsulated by hundreds of giant tree roots, at the base of a thick group of ensnarling trees that curled around it from every direction, like a giant all-encompassing hand clutching it in its palm.

The two visitors couldn't take their eyes off what they were seeing. And it occurred to the reporter that the aging structure was so enshrouded in roots and trees that even a direct hit from a hurricane wouldn't budge it.

The park ranger had explained to them that the cabin had been built long before 1936, when President Roosevelt dedicated the state park. So it and its occupants, presumably Lyle Festus' father and his son, had been given lifetime rights to live there. No one seemed to have any knowledge of a Mrs. Festus.

"Whatcha starin' at? Ain't cha never seen where a man lays his head?!"

The accusatory voice seemed to come from nowhere. Jessica and the reporter looked left and right and then straight ahead but saw no one.

And then he was practically in their faces. Like he'd literally sprung from up out of the ground.

But before Harmless or Jessica saw him, they smelled him. Because his scent was that of old, decaying wet leaves, stagnant swamp water, and, curiously, cucumbers.

Harmless had the sudden, fearful thought that he'd read somewhere that if you smell cucumbers in the woods, it's a sure sign that a copperhead lurks nearby.

But he, nonetheless, mustered enough gumption to introduce himself and Jessica. Then he explained to Festus, a solidly built man with deep creases in his leathery face and on his forehead, why they'd come so far into the forest to track him down.

"I know all about them flyin' things in the sky," Festus interrupted him. "Matter'a fact, I probably knew about 'em before y'all did. They've been flyin' all over the place here in the park for the last few weeks. I've been watchin' 'em but keepin' my distance."

"So what do you make of 'em, Mr. Festus?" Jessica asked. "Are they here just checkin' us humans out? Or do they have something else in mind?"

The old man stroked his long, dirty beard, coughed up a greenish glob of disgusting mucus from his throat, and cast his eyes upward. His raggedy, camouflaged clothes looked like they hadn't been changed in several days. Splotches of food stains (or were those from chewing tobacco?) dotted the front of his shirt.

"Well, then, they ain't no way'a knowin' the answer to that question, young lady. And anybidy tells you they knows the answer, they'd be a lyin' through their teeth.

"But I know this. If they'd meant ta' do us harm, they'd 'uv already done that. So, no, I don't think they're up to anything bad. But exactly what they're here for, who in the name of heaven really knows?"

Harmless wanted to make sure, before leaving Festus, that they'd learned all they could from him.

So he asked him straight out for his opinion of the alleged otherworldly visitors who were causing such a commotion at the beach.

"Seems like they're wantin' ta learn 'bout our wild creatures," Festus said.

"And why do you say that, Sir?" Jessica chimed in.

"Cause'a what they mighta been tryin' ta do with Tonto," Festus said.

"And who's Tonto?" Harmless asked.

"I guess you could say he's my pet alligator. Been in the family all my life, even before I was born. My daddy had 'em when I was growin' up. And guess what? He's still livin! That damned gator's pert nigh 85-years-old best I can tell."

"And where might he be right at this moment?" Jessica, her attention aroused, asked.

"Lives in a marshy pond about 8 feet deep a little over 15 minutes from here," Festus said. "I check on 'em right reg'lar like cause the old fella's slowed way down. So slow I practically have ta feed 'em to keep 'em alive. "Throw 'em a chicken ever' now an' then and he loves it. And that ain't the only thing. His teeth ain't as sharp as they once was. I'm afeard he'll get so he cain't even chew his food.

"But he still looks mean—14 feet long and with a mighty thick body. If you saw 'em, you'd damn sure keep your distance."

"So what does Tonto have ta do with what some folks believe are alien visitors in spaceships from another planet?" Jessica asked.

That's when Festus proceeded to tell them about a recent evening when he'd heard a ruckus coming from the direction of the swampy area where the old gator lived.

"It was the fish crows that got my attention. Dozens of 'em was cuttin' a shine. Not the sound of the 'caw-caw' that you're used ta' gettin' from American crows. Nope. It's more like a loud sound that you'd think was comin' from your nose. Somethin' like 'Uh-uh, Uh-uh, Uh-uh.' That's the tell-tale cry of a fish crow.

"So I commenced ta runnin' fast as I could ta Tonto's pond, and then's when I saw it."

Jessica asked, "Saw what, exactly, Mr. Festus?"

"Some livin' terrified, squirmin' somethin' between Tonto's jaws. It was fightin' ta get loose, but that old, contrary gator was fightin' just as hard to stay clamped down on it. It was thrashin' about in the water somethin' fierce, and Tonto's big thick scaly tail was slapping first one way, then another.

"And that's when that big, round, orange flyin' object landed on Tonto and somehow made him let go of what he had in his mouth.

"And then that flyin' saucer, or whatever it was, was gone, quick and as quiet as you please, and even my Tonto seemed shocked. Shoulda seen his bulgin' eyes. He reckoned he had a meal for sure, but nope, not quite. 'Cause whatever he was about to swaller got rescued, sure as I'm standin' here in these woods tellin' you about it."

Asked for his take on what the gator was chomping down on, Festus said it looked like some kind of live animal, but nothing like he'd ever seen before.

"Leastways, it didn't come from these woods. I know all the critters livin' here and there's nothin' like what I saw in Tonto's mouth. Coulda come from that flyin' saucer for all I know."

The reporter had recorded all of what Festus had told them, but when he asked if he could publish the portion about Tonto, the old man declined.

"Cause if you put that out there, these woods'ed be crawlin' with stupid folks wantin' to see an 85-year-old gator big as an old fat log. I don't want nobidy disturbin' my Tonto. Just leave 'em be. Leave 'em out of whatever you write—PLEASE."

With that, we thanked Festus for his time, wished him the best, and made our way slowly through the overhanging, thick forest back to the parking lot. It was at least a 45-minute walk, but as we got closer to the beach, we could begin to hear the ocean waves crashing up against the shore. We had only been a couple of miles into the forest, but in some ways where Festus lived had seemed like much farther away from the tell-tale signs of civilization: picnic shelters, paved roads, restrooms, campgrounds, and parking areas.

I wondered if I were an alien from another galaxy, would I really want to spend time in such a remote, hard-to-get-to-destination as a stagnant old swamp pond in the middle of a rugged, thick forest? And with a decrepit, aging reptile?

Chapter 26
A Night Out On The Town

It hadn't taken long that evening to write my article about the latest UFO sightings at the state park. I had done it from home and emailed it to my editor. True to his word, the story got priority attention on the newspaper's website, and the next day it led the news on page 1—this time boxed at the top of the page with a picture of the UFO. The story caused a stir in the community and wire services across the country picked it up.

Jessica called and congratulated me on my coverage, and I said I couldn't have done as well without her.

"Well, why don't we celebrate?" she said teasingly. "How about a night out on the town?"

"I think I've forgotten how to date anyone," I said, "but let's do it. Yes. I definitely need a night away from the paper. Pick you up at 7?"

"7 it is, Lester Harmless. And don't be late."

At the appointed time, I swung by her modest apartment near Coastal Carolina University, gave her a call, and met her at her front entrance.

"I'd invite you in but my roommate's boyfriend is here with her tonight and so they just want to be alone."

As she said this, she wrapped her arms around me, and gave me a light kiss on my left ear.

"You DO understand, don't you, Lester?"

When I said yes, she giggled and motioned for us to get going.

Jessica was radiant. Everything about her: her attractive shape, the way she was dressed (in a beguiling short skirt and matching v-cut blouse), her scent, her shiny hair which she had tied up in a bun, her smile, her alluring eyes—all of it was perfect.

How could I have been any happier or luckier?

"So where we going, big man?"

"I thought we'd hang out for a while at Fat Harold's," I said. "It's a shag dance club at North Myrtle Beach. You up for that?"

"Up for that?! Of course, I'd love to dance with you! You never told me you knew how to shag." She suddenly seemed more into this whole date night thing.

"Well, actually, I don't. But I thought maybe we could just watch and give it a try."

"I'll teach you. It's easy, Lester. Just have to shuffle your feet a little. It's kind of a two-step dance. Just follow my lead."

* * *

Forty minutes later we were at Fat Harold's, one of the oldest beach music dance clubs in North Myrtle Beach.

A beach music band called "Bob Wilson and the Fabulous Four" was playing on a slightly elevated platform next to the 20-25 couples who seemed to be thoroughly enjoying themselves on the dance floor. The band consisted of two free spirited looking guitar players, one of whom was the lead singer, a guy with a crewcut playing a saxophone, and a long-haired, hippy pounding on drums.

Jessica grabbed me by my right hand and tugged me out onto the floor.

"But I don't know what I'm doing," I protested.

"You'll do fine, Lester. Just keep your eyes on me. Watch how I move. Move the way I do."

So that's what I did.

When Jessica shuffled her feet, I tried to do the same. When she twirled, I twirled. When she grabbed me by my waist, I pulled her gently by her waist.

After a while, we sort of lost ourselves in the Carolina beach music.

It was sweet and soothing and smooth.

Not like the California surf music of the Beach Boys, but rather akin to a little bit of Jimmy Buffett and a smattering of bouncy Calypso music.

It was music you could shuffle your feet to and relax, and that's exactly what Jessica and I did.

"Just listen to the beat, Lester, and let yourself go," Jessica said to me after we'd been on the dance floor for 20 minutes. "Enjoy the sweetness and the love. Lose your soul in it."

We ended up dancing for hours, taking a break every now and then for a cold beer (a Margarita for Jessica).

Finally, it was closing time.

I took Jessica by the hand and escorted her to my car.

"Where to now, big guy?"

I told her it was to be a surprise.

"Then surprise me! Let's go!"

We got back to Myrtle Beach State Park just at closing time, but the ranger at the toll booth made an exception and let me enter. I promised him we wouldn't stay long.

Five minutes later, we were walking hand in hand on the beach.

"Look up at the sky, Jessica."

"Lester, it's lovely! There's a billion stars twinkling tonight! Like one of the most beautiful sights I've ever seen!"

"And how about that magical moonrise over the ocean?" I said. "Have you ever seen anything so stunning?"

The two of us just stood there on the beach, hand in hand, taking in all of nature's glorious handiwork.

And then I thought I heard something.

"Shush," I said. "Listen. Do you hear it?"

Jessica agreed that she did indeed seem to hear something, other than the sound of waves lapping against the shore. But what could it be? It was barely discernible, but the curious sound was definitely there.

And then we both knew.

It was the sound of heavy, labored breathing coming from a loggerhead sea turtle laying her eggs.

We must have been really close to her nest.

313

"We can hear her, but where is she?" Jessica asked.

"She's really close, maybe a lot closer than we even realize, but we won't disturb her," I said. "I've heard that out of the hundreds of eggs a sea turtle lays, only a few hatchlings survive and crawl into the ocean. Then, years later, when they themselves are ready to give birth, they come back to this exact same nest and lay their eggs. It's all a very mysterious process."

"So how do you know all that, Lester?"

I smiled and looked at the heavens.

"Let's put it this way, Jessica. You know about the planets and stars and moon, and I know a little about sea turtles."

We strolled a bit farther down the beach, and I thought I heard the faint crackling of thunder.

"I guess we better haul out of here," I told her. "I promised that ranger we wouldn't be long."

Suddenly, she threw her arms around me, held me tightly, and locked her luscious lips on mine.

Larry C. Timbs Jr.

All I could think about, at that very moment, was that Jessica Perry and I were meant to be together.

We stayed there, holding and kissing one another in the moonlight on the beach for five minutes. It was a tender, intimate moment that we didn't want to end. And then we parted, but not before promising to come back to this very same spot in the near future.

"Because we heard that loggerhead turtle for a reason, Lester. I think we're destined to return here."

On that note, we gave each other a high five.

I smiled, took her hand, and we walked back down the beach. We made it through the sea oats and up the dunes and back to my car.

It had been a perfect evening, and all I could think about was the future. Maybe OUR future? But who could predict such things? I said a silent prayer to myself that she wouldn't get bored with me and that I'd have a chance to romance her many more starry nights.

***

315

At my bungalow, after I'd dropped Jessica off at her apartment, I was exhausted. It had been a long but immensely good, memorable day. I had actually been on a date, with a woman who seemed to care about me and what I did for a living.

It had been way too long since I'd been out with anyone. Because, for one thing, my job was all consuming. It never let up— at no time of the day or night. News always happened, and regardless of what my journalism job description said, I had to answer the call whenever I was summoned.

Such was the nature of the profession I had chosen.

Just then my cell phone rang.

I didn't recognize the number and so was tempted not to answer.

But who on earth could be calling me at this time of the night—at 1:30 in the morning? And what could they possibly want?

I didn't pick up but the ringing persisted.

Aggravated and tired but curious, I answered.

"Mr. Harmless, you gotta come right now."

I asked to whom I was talking.

"It's Digger Elliott. I'm at the cemetery. Spending the night in my van again. You gotta see this to believe it."

"Mr. Elliott, it's almost 2 in the morning. This can't wait till tomorrow?"

"I'm afeard they'll be gone by then. Come right now! You'll get yourself a helluva story."

Then he hung up.

It took me about 20 minutes to drive to Pleasant Grove Cemetery. The place was deathly dark, with only a few solar lights placed here and there along pathways winding through the graveyard.

Didn't take me long to locate the gravedigger's beat up old van. It was parked under an overhanging limb from a huge live oak tree.

Elliott saw my headlights and walked to meet me.

"It's over there!" he shouted, turning and pointing behind him.

"What's over there? What you talking about?"

317

"See for yourself, Mr. Harmless. Seein's believin'!"

So I began walking in the direction he pointed and then, after about 10 yards, stopped suddenly.

Finally, there it was. A creature, being, thing—whatever you wanted to call it—only a few feet from me.

So incredibly strange and mysterious and like nothing I'd ever seen.

Definitely from another world.

More globular, ghastly shaped than obvious substance.

But, after getting over my initial shock, I could tell there WAS substance of some sort within that vapory mist.

At first, I thought an armless and legless body of some kind?

But the more I stared, my take on it changed.

I noticed, for example, two giant glistening black orbs in the upper part of the shape that seemed locked, if you will, on my eyes.

318

And yes—now I thought I detected some sort of thin hideous looking appendages. They were moving ever so slightly, as if fingering the air, and they were attached to very long impossibly thin limbs.

And now, just barely, I could make out the head—huge and not round but rather geometrically triangular with those two dark black orbs staring right through me.

But it had absolutely no nose, no mouth, and no lips.

And a wafer-thin wrinkly neck supported its head.

So different. So very bizarre. Couldn't have imagined it if I'd wanted to.

And then, taking me completely by surprise, it extended one of its thin appendages—its limbs if you will—toward me.

What to do when an alien, hopefully a friendly one, makes an overture toward you? Wallow in fear? Run? Yell desperately for help? Kneel down and pray?

After a few seconds, I extended my right hand and touched it.

It was like touching nothing I'd ever come in contact with.

Not human but not like an animal or any other alive thing either. More like, well, let's just say it wasn't of this world.

So icy, deathly cold I couldn't have maintained bodily contact with it even if I'd wanted to.

It made no sound whatsoever, but I was certain that it knew I was afraid.

And it seemed to be trying to reassure me that it wasn't there to harm me. But instead just to observe and learn and take in what it must have been: an entirely different, strange life form.

So there I was—face to face with what had to be not of this world.

Behind me, I could hear the rustling sound of Digger Elliott closing his van doors.

He yelled to me, "Are you okay, Mr. Harmless? Should I call the police?"

"No need," I answered. "Whatever this thing is, it's not here to hurt us."

And then, quite gradually, the creature began to back away from me. It made a waving motion (goodbye?) with one of its thin spindly arms and then dissolved into the dark mist of the night.

"Whadya goin' ta do now?" the gravedigger asked me.

"I don't know," Mr. Elliott. "Did you get a picture of it?"

"My cell phone camera don't work. I'm sorry. Been meanin' ta get a new phone but just cain't swing it just yet."

"It's okay," I said. "Nobody'd believe us anyway."

Chapter 27
Unfinished Business At The Cemetery

I didn't sleep well at all that night. What was it, exactly, that I had encountered? An alien from another world? Just a hallucination on my part? I didn't think so, but I had to admit I'd been under a lot of stress, and UFOs had been on my mind a lot the last few weeks.

I decided right then and there just to keep the encounter with the creature to myself. It would serve no useful purpose, I figured, to arouse a bunch of extraterrestrial skeptics, or, possibly worse, to invite attention from fanatical believers.

It was just Miles Elliott and me who'd witnessed the creature, and who would believe a lowly, common gravedigger?

I had to pinch myself to keep from laughing out loud, comparing the believability and integrity of a professional journalist to that of a man who dug graves for a living.

Perhaps, after all, we weren't that much different. Because we both performed a necessary public service, one that was taken for granted all too often. We both were paid a pittance (relatively speaking) and we could easily anger or antagonize people even when we're trying our level best to do a good job. I imagined that Mr. Elliott had on occasion imbibed a little too much alcohol, and it showed up in a defectively carved out grave.

Early that following morning after my night encounter with the creature at Pleasant Grove Cemetery, I had made myself a strong cup of black coffee, had a quick bowl of cereal, and hightailed it down to the beach.

It was 6 a.m. and I had the beach to myself. Far as I could see, there were no other humans—only seagulls hanging in the ocean breeze and pelicans bobbing among the waves. The latter reminded me of a cute little poetic snippet:

A curious bird is the pelican.
His beak holds more than his belly can.

I waded to where the waves gently sloshed up against the shore and put my bare feet in the ocean.

The cold ocean salt water seemed to massage and sooth my feet.

Rivulets of the ocean ran between my toes and up to just slightly above my ankles. The packed wet sand felt fabulous on my feet and especially so when I crinkled my toes.

The overall feeling was one of restoration and rejuvenation.

And soon enough, there on the horizon, a huge glowing, glorious red ball—about 93 million miles from our planet, I'm told—announced the dawn of a new day.

Standing there on the shore, looking out over the blue-green ocean and at the swaying palm trees just beyond the dune in back of me, it occurred to me that there were far worse places to be than Myrtle Beach, South Carolina. And surely much less enchanting.

I made a pact to myself right then and there, that regardless of what happened with my future at the paper or with the UFOs or anything else, I would not leave this place.

As I turned to leave, my cell phone rang.

I didn't recognize the number but the phone said the call originated from Pleasant Grove Cemetery. "Hello. Lester Harmless here."

It was none other than Jefferson Aller, superintendent of the cemetery. I had met him briefly a few weeks earlier when I had tried to get in contact with Miles Elliott. And I had seen him at the exhumation court proceeding, where he had appeared but had not been called upon to testify.

Our phone conversation started out on a curious note.

"Mr. Harmless, I couldn't live with myself any longer without talking to you. Something extremely bothersome has happened at the cemetery and I figured you had a right to know about it. But I'd prefer not to tell you on the phone. Can you come to my office at once?"

I asked him if it pertained to UFOs and he gave me a noncommittal but lukewarm yes.

He added: "You'll have to determine that after you hear what I have to say."

Within an hour, I was sitting in a high-backed wooden chair in his office. He rose to shake hands, directly across from me, before taking a seat behind his massive desk.

He had on a black suit coat, a black tie, and dark grey pants. And I noticed a thick black walking cane, a serpent's head carved on the end where he held it, propped up in one corner of his office.

One of the first things I noticed about him was the tiny bronze coffin on his left lapel.

He was a striking figure, well over 6 feet tall, and extremely pale, as if he'd been out of the sunlight for quite some time. His hair, like his skin and even his lips, was white, and his hands were bony, long, and cold. *He himself could have just crawled out of a coffin.*

A plaque hanging on his office wall had his engraved name along with the citation: FOR OUTSTANDING SERVICE TO HUMANITY— PRESENTED TO JEFFERSON P. ALLER BY THE SOUTH CAROLINA CEMETERY ASSOCIATION.

In a corner of his office, stacked up against the wall, were two silver-plated shovels.

"Thank you for agreeing to come see me on such short notice," he said. "But it's a matter that's been on my mind for quite some time. I should have gotten in touch with you much sooner."

That got my attention.

As did the miniature horse drawn wagon—its cargo a coffin—sitting squarely in front of him at the edge of his desk.

"Before I get to the reason for meeting with you today, a few words about my background. I've been in the business of taking care of corpses, deceased bodies, souls, remains—whatever you want to call them—for quite some time. In fact, I'd say I've been dealing with the dead for longer than you've been in this world."

He smiled slightly and I noticed just a tinge of pinkness on his lips and perhaps a hint of the same in his eyes. Could this pallid man be some sort of aberrant half-breed albino?

"I've worked in just about every facet of the funeral profession," he continued. "From being a funeral director and owning a funeral home to running a crematorium. From being a mortician and embalming bodies and now to being in charge of a cemetery where I have responsibility for two-thousand resting souls. I've even been known, in a crunch, to help dig a grave or assist in the placement of a tombstone.

"What I'm saying is this: when it comes to caring for the dead and for their grieving, suffering families, I've done it. It's been more of a lifetime calling and honor than simply an occupation, although I'll have to admit I've made a good living."

He paused to let what he'd said sink in.

"You're probably thinking, as I speak, that I've chosen a profession that is somehow creepy or dark, and you may even think of me as such. But let me assure you, young man, that what I do is an essential service. We, and that includes you, will all die one day. So sooner or later—and let us hope that it's much later—you will need my services."

As he spoke, he pushed a small business card across his desk toward me.

"Just in case," he said.

"Now that I've told you a bit about myself and what I've done, let's get to the needle."

"The needle?" I wondered aloud.

"Not to worry," he said, smiling. "It's an old undertaker's expression. I'm not going to stick you, but I do have a point in summoning you here today. "It has to do with a dog, actually. A frisky, very smart, border collie named Doodles. The dog's owner was Mrs. Linda Sue Dickinson. I think you may have met her husband?"

"Yes," I said. "Mr. Randolph Dickinson had his late wife buried here in your cemetery."

"You are correct, Sir," he said. "Well, it seems that Ms. Robin Jones took ownership of Doodles when her sister passed away. And Ms. Jones would bring the dog to the cemetery when she visited her sister's gravesite. Nothing unusual there. Survivors often bring pets to visit the gravesites of their human masters."

"So then, what struck you as odd?" I asked.

"It's just that after that supposed flying saucer sighting—you know the one by my employee Miles Elliott—Doodles behaved much differently."

"How so?"
"Up until the time of the reported sighting, each time Ms. Jones visited her sister's gravesite, her dog would lie down there, its ears drooping and

rest its head on the ground. And there it would stay, even for more than an hour if Ms. Jones remained in the cemetery that long, until she left. "What I'm saying is this. Ms. Jones could walk around and look at other headstones and take in the giant oak trees and our other beautiful, peaceful surroundings, and Doodles would not leave the gravesite of Mrs. Dickinson. It was actually quite astonishing to see the emotional attachment Doodles still had for her late master.

"Not that I haven't seen this before. I surely have. Animals have a sixth sense about them. Many times they will linger for long periods of time at a burial site, hoping that their human master returns for them. Some experts believe they can still pick up the scent of their buried humans, especially if they weren't embalmed. And some believe that even if they were embalmed, a canine's sense of smell is many hundred times over more keen than that of a human.

"Now, personally speaking, I'm not an expert, but I have seen a thing or two, and I believe, as sure as I'm sitting here in my office with you, that Doodles smelled his human master each time that dog visited the gravesite. But everything changed after my gravedigger, Miles Elliott, said that flying saucer hovered over her grave."

"Meaning exactly how or what, Sir?" I asked.

"Meaning that AFTER Mr. Elliott's flying saucer report, Ms. Jones would still bring Doodles with her to the cemetery but the dog no longer felt a deep emotional attachment to Mrs. Dickinson's gravesite. The animal would trot over to the grave with Ms. Jones but would not remain there. In my humble opinion, Doodles could no longer pick up the scent of her master's human remains. That could be because, well, I don't want to speculate, but possibly..."

He didn't finish the sentence but instead just left me hanging there to surmise or speculate. *Could it have been that Doodles, the very intelligent dog, no longer hung around the gravesite because Mrs. Dickinson's corpse was no longer buried there?*

"So what you're suggesting, Sir, is that the body of the late Linda Sue Dickinson no longer rests in the grave where she was placed?"

"Not at all, but what I'm getting at is that I'm NOT suggesting that what you're saying is inaccurate," he responded.

What to make of that kind of ambiguous, vague doubletalk?

I tried to pin him down, to no avail.

Instead, he became borderline impertinent, said he had a long list of duties to perform that same day and bid me farewell.

"But Sir," I protested. "You can't leave me hanging like that. Just a few more questions."

"I said that's all, Mr. Harmless. I've spoken my piece. Cleared my conscience. Shared what has bothered me for several weeks and even caused me to lose sleep. So that's it. I have three burials to plan for tomorrow. Good day and good luck."

Chapter 28
A Parting Gift

Jefferson Aller, superintendent of the Pleasant Grove Cemetery, had given me a lot to think about, to say the least.

What to make of Doodles the dog always lying down on his master's grave? And then, after the flying saucer had made a visit there, the dog no longer smelled Linda Sue Dickinson's corpse?

Or was that just something that happened a lot with dogs? Maybe, for reasons we humans would never fathom, a dog could sense where his master was—dead or alive. But how would we ever know for sure what Doodles knew or didn't know? It all made for fascinating conjecture and head scratching but no definitive answers were forthcoming.

Because dogs, regardless of how intelligent they are, do not talk.

So I tried to put Doodles and the extremely pallid caretaker of the cemetery out of my mind. But the more I thought about the latter, he reminded me of a vampire.

But, of course, he didn't have fangs (that I knew of) and wasn't several hundred years old. And surely, for all his weirdness, he didn't sleep in a crypt and turn into a vicious werewolf (or worse) at midnight.

Or did he?

I forced myself to quit thinking about him and checked my office phone messages.

"Lester, this is Rose. You might remember a woman named Lucille Mulligan. I believe you wrote about her as being one of the three local women who were abducted several weeks ago by creatures in a UFO. Well, she has died, and the editor thinks her death is worthy of more than just a run of the mill obituary. He wants you to track down her next of kin and write a story about her."

The message from the all-knowing Rose Jansen, news clerk of the Ocean Herald, was polite enough, but beneath that politeness I could sense that this just wasn't a friendly FYI. It was my current assignment to begin pursuing as soon as possible. So I emailed Rose to thank her and let her know I was on it.

I did some quick research on the internet and found some basic preliminary funeral information about Lucille Mulligan. She had just died at an early age, only 58 years old. No cause of death was listed, and only one survivor, her husband for the last 25 years was noted. His name was Kenneth T. Mulligan. The funeral home announcement gave his place of employment as Jack Kress Towing and Auto Repair of Murrells Inlet.

It was a quick drive to the auto repair place but a grease-covered worker there quickly informed me that it was Kenneth's day off and "if he ain't in the marsh fishin' or tryin' to catch crabs, you'll git 'em at his trailer."

"And where might that be," I asked.

"Just follow this here road," he said, motioning to the pot-hole filled two-lane pavement in front of the auto repair shop, till you get to tha third light. Take a right there and go two lights and hang a left. You'll see a bunch of run-down trailers in the weeds. His'en's the one with the big blue stripe runnin' down the middle of it. And watch your step when you walk up on his porch. That damned thing is rotten ta the core."

I found the place with little trouble and rapped on the screen door. (The regular door was wide open). I could see through the patched screen door that Kenneth T. Mulligan had a cold, frothy beer in his right hand and was reclining on a stained and torn sofa that had seen better days.

"Go away! I ain't wantin' nothin' that you're sellin,' Mister," he shouted.

"Sir, I'm not here to sell you anything. I'm a reporter for the Ocean Herald. I just want to ask you a few questions about your wife."

"What's there to say? She's dead as a door nail! I done seen her body yesterday. Gonna' have her buried tomorrow. And ain't havin' no autopsy. Ain't wantin' nobidy to cut her up like a frog!"

"I'm sorry for your loss, Sir," I said, still standing outside and talking to him through the duct-taped, held-together screen door. "May I come in just for a few minutes?" I was suddenly mindful of that caution I'd been given about his rotting porch.

"The door ain't locked," he said.

He guzzled the rest of his beer and wiped his mouth with his hairy right forearm.

Even though it was apparently his day off from the auto repair place, his clothes looked to be oily and dirty. He had on blue work pants, the kind you often see worn by auto mechanics, and a light blue short-sleeved shirt, with his name "Kenneth" in cursive above his left shirt pocket. In that same pocket I could see the top of a package of Marlboro cigarettes.

"Now, what you wantin' ta know about my wife Lucille?"

I asked him to tell me about her, and he said there wasn't much to tell. She had been a good, loyal wife for all the years they'd been married, had kept him straight (not an easy thing) and never bothered nobidy.

As to why she had just died, at such an early age, he said there was no doubt about it. She had absolutely been tormented to death by the flying saucer that she and her two friends, Maxine Robinson and Ida Mae James, had encountered on that lonely stretch of highway on their way back home from a late-night outing.

"I mean ta tell ya, she was never tha same after that," the man said. He fetched another beer from the fridge, popped the top, and took a big swig, leaving a swath of white foam from his chin up to his nose.

"I never did know what ta think to be honest with ya, but I know my Lucille never told a fib in her whole life. Why, she didn't know how ta lie.

"But folks wouldn't leave her be. They kept pesterin' her and some said she was makin' the whole thing up just ta draw attention.

"But my Lucille weren't like that a'tall. She never wanted ta be famous. Just wanted ta be left alone ta live her life and take care a' me. Which can be a full-time job, if ya know what I mean, Mister? Me bein' always strugglin' to put food on our table and keep my job."

As he spoke about his wife, I walked around the small, paneled living room, and that's when I noticed it: an unframed painting of a flying saucer hanging in a corner of the room. The spaceship appeared to be a huge, disc-shaped, domed object. Small, illuminated windows appeared on its side as it hovered above an old car. A passenger in the car was leaning out of a side window and staring upward, mouth wide open and eyes entranced in wonder, at the object.

I stood spellbound, unable to take my eyes off the painting.

"What is this?" I asked.

"It's a picture of that damned thing that killed her," Kenneth Mulligan said angrily.

"So your wife painted this?"

When he assured me that she had, I told him that it was indeed a rare treasure to have a painting of a UFO.

"So, do you want it then?" he asked me.

I said, "Yes." He took the painting down from the wall and gave it to me which I gratefully accepted and which, unbeknownst by me at the time, I would treasure for the rest of my life.

Because I figured I had an object of art that was beautiful and mysterious. Something that very few people had: an actual eyewitness-created painting of a flying saucer.

A short time later, I completed my story about the curious death of Lucille Mulligan, and the piece ran on the front page under the 48-point headline

"Why Did She Die?" And of course the folks in the graphic arts department took great delight in boxing my story with a picture of Lucille's painting of the UFO.

The package did what the newspaper wanted it to do: keep UFOs front and center with readers at Myrtle Beach. We sold so many papers that our press run had to be increased. That edition of the Ocean Herald became a collector's item.

But for me, I was just mainly glad to have stumbled upon a tangible piece of what I considered to be priceless memorabilia; whether you believed in them or not, flying saucers had forever left their marks on our community, and now I had a physical reminder that I could always hold on to.

My friend Jessica couldn't believe my good fortune.

"So her husband just actually gave that portrait to you? Didn't he understand what his wife had left him?"

She then made me promise that I'd have it suitably framed, which I did, and that I'd never let it change hands.

"What you have, Lester, is something exquisite, and very special. You could even say it depicts something from another world. No one, and I mean no one, should ever make you second guess that. Promise me that you'll always hold on to it."

Chapter 29
The Beat Goes On

The next morning dawned like any other day on the Grand Strand. A glorious big red sun ball peeked over the horizon at a little before 7. And you could smell a refreshing salty breeze from the ocean. Although I was not at the beach, I could still picture the waves—forever sloshing up against the sandy, seemingly endless shoreline. Slowly eating away more of the land and replacing it with the sea.

I had the day off so it was a good time to recharge, meditate, and just kick back and relax. No thoughts today of flying saucers, creatures from billions of miles away, court disputes, or police investigations.

Or at least I tried not to think of such.

But a journalist's mind always is preoccupied with something he's written about or observed. Because that's what we do most every day of our lives. We observe people and things and happenings and try to capture them in words.

It occurred to me that this whole ordeal with the UFOs over the last several weeks had kept me preoccupied. To the extent that I'd almost lost sight of what else was happening on the Grand Strand.

But the rhythms of predictable, everyday life at Myrtle Beach had continued, just as they always had and always would.

As the weather got warmer, the beaches would become more "peopled." Already, the days were consistently hitting the mid to high 80s, and when that happened, as sure as the sun rose, humans would make their way to the ocean.

Anywhere on the coast to relax, sunbathe, and forget about the humdrum routines of the work world.

That meant, for tens of thousands of folks each late spring and throughout the summer, piling into their cars and heading for Myrtle Beach.

They would come from just about everywhere, especially from all over the Carolinas, Tennessee, and Virginia, but also from as far away as Ohio, Pennsylvania, New Jersey, New York, Connecticut, Vermont, Maine, and even Canada.

Such was the enchanting, eternal pull of our coastal community.

And when they got to the beach, you'd see them loading what seemed to me to be half their possessions and dragging them down to the ocean. Because a day at the beach wouldn't be fun not having a comfortable chair to stretch out in, or not having a nice big umbrella to keep you shielded from the scorching sun. And, of course, you had to have a cooler full of cold refreshments and sandwiches, towels, beach toys for the littles, a radio to keep you entertained, books or magazines...and the list went on and on.

I smiled, thinking of all the husbands and boyfriends I'd noticed at the beach looking like overburdened mules. It wasn't easy getting all that "essential" stuff to where you planned to spend the day by the ocean. But the lifting, loading, and dragging helped keep your wife, girlfriend, or family happy.

Tourism was the heartbeat of the economy on the Grand Strand.

And, of course, the heartbeat of the heartbeat was the beach.

Because without the beach, hardly anyone would come here.

And not that Myrtle Beach didn't have problems.

Because in 2022, the signs welcoming all those visitors to our fair community might as well have said:

"Welcome To Beautiful Myrtle Beach—home of honking horns, high gas and food prices, congested roadways, labor shortages in motels and restaurants, and a building boom that's threatening all of us."

Still, however, the people would continue to come here.

Whatever it costs, they would pay.

Thousands of dollars for a small, bare bones apartment, or $6 for one scoop of ice cream near the beach? $40 a day to rent a beach umbrella?

They'd gladly pay.

Houses here that had sold for $250,000 just three years ago selling today for $450,000?! Home insurance premiums getting obscenely higher every year because this was hurricane country?! No problem.

People intent on living permanently at Myrtle Beach would fork out whatever it took to get them into a home.

A growing resentment, from the locals, that overpopulation and overdevelopment of the Grand Strand was straining an already stressed and aging infrastructure.

Who really gave a rat's behind?

Especially if you were from up North, had sold your home there, and now had a fat bank account that allowed you to buy whatever place you wanted at the beach.

Those who were already residents of the beach, from the North or elsewhere, were staying smugly put in their homes, even though they could make a killing if they sold them. They were comfortably dug in, living "inside their piggy banks" of fastly-appreciating-in-value properties, and enjoying the good life in "this little corner of paradise," as some folks put it. So, at Myrtle Beach they intended to take their last breaths.

Never mind that not all was as good as it could be in this place where so many had decided to spend their hard-earned dollars.

My cell phone pinged, alerting me to a text message.

It was from the news clerk of the Ocean Herald.

I breathed a sigh of relief when I read it and discovered it was not about covering another UFO sighting. Those had become far fewer of late, and I wondered if our visitors from outer space had decided they'd had quite enough of Myrtle Beach.

No, this particular message was directing me to a special event at the Myrtle Beach Rotary Club the next day. The Rotarians were planning to present a Police Officer of the Year award.

The award, according to the message, was named after one Joseph McGarry, a Myrtle Beach police officer who died in the line of duty in late December 2002.

I did some quick research and learned that McGarry, 28 at the time of his death, had been at a Myrtle Beach Dunkin' Doughnuts on North Kings Highway when he noticed a man who he thought might have committed a crime. He had exited the restaurant to question the man when the suspect had suddenly turned and shot him in the face with a 45-calibre pistol.

McGarry hadn't had time to draw his own firearm, but his partner managed to shoot the guy in the leg, wounding him enough so that he could be arrested. The shooter had been languishing all these years on Death Row in a South Carolina prison.

So the award the Rotarians would present was obviously intended to help keep officer McGarry's legacy alive.

A good story that I would enjoy covering.

So I texted Rose, the news clerk, that I was on it.

And no sooner had I texted her than I got a text from the beleaguered Randolph Dickinson. He said he'd felt completely let down by the local court system and wondered if there was anything else I or he could do to get his wife's body exhumed.

I considered telling him about the border collie that no longer obviously could smell Linda Sue Dickinson's corpse, but then thought better of it.

What, after all, did any of that situation with the dog actually prove? What judge would run with that and grant a new exhumation hearing?

It would do no good, I decided, to bring the dog up. Nope, not at all. Only thing it'd do is give Mr. Dickinson false hope.

So I texted him back and promised him (a bit of a white lie on my part) I'd stay alert for any new developments and keep him posted.

To which he didn't reply, thankfully.

Next, I called the newsroom to see if there'd been any breaking developments with regard to UFOs— at Myrtle Beach or elsewhere.

An overworked, irritable assistant editor took my call and said that "all's been quiet regarding flying saucers the last few days and you'll be the first to know if that changes."

Then there was a click when he hung up suddenly without even saying goodbye.

Overworked, stretched thin, and underpaid just like everyone else in the newsroom, I figured.

Typical.

Sometimes, I wondered if I'd chosen the right profession. Because journalism had such a short, impatient attention span.

UFOs—front and center on the news agenda for weeks at Myrtle Beach—were now, it seemed, relegated as an afterthought.

And they wouldn't be covered again, by me or anyone else at the Ocean Herald, unless someone credible saw one.

And when might that be?

Only whatever or whoever was flying in those spaceships could answer that key question.

Meanwhile, breaking news still percolated by the second, it seemed, and I had plenty to keep me busy or at least to think about.

Russian soldiers had committed unspeakable war crimes against women and children and other civilians in Ukraine.

An Alabama corrections officer had helped a convicted murderer escape from prison, and the two of them (the female officer and inmate) had been on the lam for more than a week.

A body, thought to be that of a 17-year-old high school girl missing on the Grand Strand since 2009, had been found in an alligator-infested swamp about 25 miles south of Myrtle Beach.

An interstellar meteor, a chunk of space rock from far beyond our solar system, had crashed on our planet, causing quite a stir in the space community.

An 18-year-old white supremacist had murdered 10 African-Americans at a grocery store in Buffalo, New York.

Likewise, another 18-year-old, armed with an AR-15, had penetrated the security of an elementary school in Uvalde, Texas, and killed 19 students and two teachers.

And last, but not least, something fascinating called the "Galileo Project" had been started by a team of researchers at Harvard, Princeton, Cambridge, and Stockholm universities. The purpose of the project was to probe interstellar space for evidence of extraterrestrial life, something that if found would have "huge implications on society (and on) humanity," according to one of the scientists at Harvard.

That last story, I decided, might be a good way for me to segue into an article updating the status of UFOs at the beach.

So maybe I'd end up writing about what the future might hold when it came to UFOs. I thought of my astronomy professor contact at Coastal Carolina University. He'd surely have something to say about what they were doing on the UFO front at Harvard.

But that was for another time.

Today was mine. Just to do with it what I wanted.

I set out for the beach at Myrtle Beach State Park, one of my favorite haunts where you could do absolutely nothing and still feel like you'd accomplished something great for yourself.

Epilogue

As I put the finishing touches on this book, an intelligence committee in the United States Congress was holding public hearings on unidentified aerial phenomena (UAP).

So we've come a long way from 1947 and Roswell, New Mexico.

The purpose of the government hearings is to open up to the public exactly what our government knows about mysterious objects that no one—not aviators, not air traffic controllers, not experts at the Pentagon on interstellar space, not the best minds in science—has yet been able to identify.

The federal government has pledged to be as transparent as possible, meaning it will disclose to the public all that it knows about UFOs, as long as such disclosure does not potentially damage our national security.

Meanwhile, at last count, as I wrote this in mid-2022, some 400 unexplained UAP encounters had been documented in the skies above the United States from 2004-2021. And, if current trends continue, that number is bound to increase.

The question always, of course, is where exactly are the objects coming from. And what are their intentions?

A corollary question is when will we earthlings make indisputable contact with the "aliens"—if indeed this is what they are. It's always possible, some people have asserted, that the so-called extraterrestrials are actually manifestations of extremely advanced, secret technology from a U.S. adversary such as China or Russia.

But if the objects are indeed piloted by aliens from another world, I would say we are getting closer to meeting them.

That they exist is almost a given.

I say "almost" because there are still those who'll call you crazy for even suggesting that we are not alone in this vast universe. It's the historic stigma attached to believers in extraterrestrials.

But I beg to differ, and that's one of the reasons for this book.

One small piece of "evidence" to bolster what I'm saying.

Hanging in my home is a beautiful portrait of a flying saucer. It was painted by an eyewitness to a famous UFO in the late 1970s.

She, along with two other women, swore that they were abducted by creatures in a UFO on a lonely stretch of rural highway.

Their story inspired the writing of this novel.

My take: we humans are not alone.

About the Author

Larry C. Timbs Jr. is a USAF veteran and retired university journalism professor.

He is the co-author, with Michael Manuel, of two novels: "Fish Springs: Beneath the Surface" (2014) and "Justice for Toby" (2016).

He is also the author of "Unlikeliest Witness: An Appalachian Story of Suspense" (2018) and "From the Beak of an Eagle: Memoirs of a Winthrop Faculty Member" (2021).

"Harmless News in Myrtle Beach: A Journalist Seeks the Truth About UFOs" (2022) is his fifth book.

He lives three miles from the ocean in Surfside Beach, South Carolina with his wife Patsy, his dog Jackson, and their cat Jake. Ever faithful and beloved companion Joe, the writer's other dog, passed away as this book was sent to the publisher.

He can be reached at larrytimbs@gmail.com.

www.ingramcontent.com/pod-product-compliance
Lightning Source LLC
Chambersburg PA
CBHW051227260626
47162CB00002B/300